The Greek Constellations – Aquarius

The Greek Constellations – Aquarius

Stephan De Jonghe

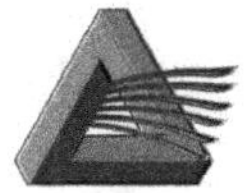

Contents

In the foot-steps of Homer and Hesiod

From Astronomy to Mythology
How the constellations came to be named by the Greek
God's.

Stephan De Jonghe

Book Eleven

The constellation - Aquarius

The story of Ganymede the Water Bearer

The Greek Constellations – Aquarius

by Stephan De Jonghe

ISBN 978-1-7636516-8-5 (paperback)
ISBN 978-1-7636516-9-2 (Ebook)

Publisher
Stephan De Jonghe Publishing,
Hillarys, Perth, Western Australia, Australia 6025

Printer and distributor
Ingram Content Group
1 Ingram Blvd.
La Vergne, Tennessee USA 37086

The dedication

To say that my darling wife is the love of my life
is an understatement.

Deb is my best friend, soul mate, confidant, and life partner.

Among so many other things, we also share a love of books, and
we have a massive library on display in our home of books that we
want to read.

Our topics include action, comedy, romance, science fiction,
crime, thrillers, and adventure.
We also have an impressive non-fiction collection.

My endeavours as an author represent a passion that
burns powerfully for me. I am driven to write.

I have many stories to tell and writing them and publishing them
is my way of contributing to other people's library's.

Writing involves many hours of research and then sitting in soli-
tude, slowly assembling the words that details a journey into a read-
able story. One that was only previously an idea.

This takes a lot of patience and persistence.
After the story is put down, the process of editing begins.

Few non-writers understand that this stage can take as much five times longer than it takes to write the actual first draft.

My Deb gives me the support that I need to execute my writing passion.
She not only supports my writing, but also enjoys reading the stories.

Her assistance with proof reading, feed-back on content, and editing, is invaluable.
Especially after I have become blind to my own errors.
She understands how important it is to me and to you, the reader, to get it right.

I dedicate these books to my wife as my thanks to her for her on-going support, and for her contributions to the finished publications.

We are a team.

We both hope that you enjoy this series of books,
and we look forward to your feedback.

Stephan and Deb De Jonghe

Special thanks

My special thanks go to Janey Emery – Renowned Australian artist, for giving me permission to use her art for the covers for my Greek Constellation series of books.

"I hope you enjoy her art and the story within these pages."
Stephan De Jonghe - Author

Janey's Story - Born in Narrogin, Western Australia, Janey Emery's interest in art began as early as 2 years of age and led to art becoming the central element in Janey's Childhood. Excelling in art throughout her school years Janey devoted herself to the art course provided by Balcatta Senior High school, where her passion for art only intensified.

Janey has been painting fulltime since 1991 and has attained a high degree of respect in the art world from peers and art lovers alike. Janey has won numerous distinguished artistic awards for her work and has sold many paintings throughout Australia and overseas. Janey Emery is achieving the recognition her distinctive artistic talents deserve.

Janey is Self-Taught in All Mediums with the exception of leisure courses undertaken in oil and water colours.

"Art has always played a part of who I am. From early childhood to now there has been a need for me to express myself through drawing and painting. I find peace in my craft, and I hope I bring that to my paintings."

"To me, my Art is like breathing. Painting is my life."
Janey Emery - Artist
https://www.janeyemery.art/

Author's note

This story is based on Greek mythology. The word Aquarius however, is Latin for Water Bearer. Many thousands of years ago, the origin of the constellation Aquarius was one of the stories imagined by ancient travellers and sailors.

Many of these stories owe some of their earlier history to the Phoenicians, Babylonians, and Mycenaean's, and they were initially used to help ancient travellers remember star patterns as a nighttime navigational tool. Over time, these fascinating stories were greatly embellished on how the constellations came to be formed. The ancient Greeks called these constellations the "Katasterismoi" meaning, "the placing of the stars." They gave names and told stories about forty-eight out of the eighty-eight constellations that are recognised by the International Astronomical Union.

These mythologies were embellished as they were countlessly re-told with tales of gods encountering wild creatures, fighting fierce battles, and of course having lots of sex. After all, these men were away from home for lengthy periods of time. They shared these stories to entertain urban dwellers that they encountered, and from there, the stories became legends, and for many people they became their religion.

A Greek poet and storyteller named Homer, was the first person to document these stories and he is most famous for the "Iliad" and the "Odyssey" which he composed some 2,800 years ago. Whilst little is known about Homer, he is regarded by many as the founder of modern literature. His two main works were the first literary works to be taught formally to students.

Interestingly, there are thirty-three film adaptations of the Odyssey, proving his works are still relevant to modern audiences.

Later, a poet named Hesiod, significantly contributed to Greek mythology and followed on from Homer's work. Together they are attributed with establishing ancient Greek religious customs, formal astronomy, the development of structured learning, documenting events, early economics, commercial farming, and time keeping.

The word "zodiac" originated from the Greek words "Zodiakos kuklos," meaning "circle of little animals". It wasn't until 50BCE that the first classical zodiac depicting the twelve astrological star signs in their current order was first depicted. It is known as the "Dendera zodiac."

During the 2nd century CE, a Greco-Roman astrologer and astronomer named Claudius Ptolemy worked on his documented Tetrabiblos into what is regarded as western astrology's primary source document and remains largely in use today. Also of note is that astronomers have named a crater on the Luna surface, and another on the surface of the planet Mars Ptolemaeus, in honour of Ptolemy and his contribution to astronomy.

The connection between Greek names and Roman names for the same deities came from their translation from one language to the other. In ancient Greek, Zeus is pronounced Dias. In Latin that became Djous Pater (Sky father) or Luppiter. In English this became Jupiter. Many names evolved in this way.

As an author, my goal is to turn what is known of the mythology, into an enjoyable story for today's reader.

Stephan De Jonghe

Chronology

Yet another note from the author, Stephan De Jonghe

My "from astronomy to mythology" series of novellas posed some difficulties in terms of writing the stories into a logical chronology. Until the Iliad, and the Odessey, no one had ever written any of the tales of titan's forming the world, or their ultimate defeat by the gods who eventually resided in Mount Olympus. These stories were imagined piecemeal, embellished, refined, and retold over a thousand-year period. Unlike history, which did happen on a linear timeline and can be plotted, the timeline used in fictional stories were not relevant, and by their very nature at the whim of the storyteller. Over the millennia, re-tellers of the stories frequently added details, and characters that were often inconsistent with the other stories. No one knew and no one cared, as they were mostly just for entertainment.

For the more serious devotees, these stories were the basis for a religion, and many aspects of the stories were used to focus worshippers' attention, and they were therefore treated by many at the time as historical facts. They focused their attention on those gods and goddesses that were consistent with their beliefs and values.

The best example that I can use to demonstrate the challenge of chronology, is referencing a main character known as Pandora. As she is the first human woman, she features in her own story, but she was created by Hephaestus, the son of Zeus and Hera, and it happened when Zeus and Hera were already married. But Zeus met and fell in love with Europa, a human woman, who was alive before he married

Hera, and before he had a son to ask to make the first woman. Challenging!

As an author with a particular attention to detail, (at least I believe I do), the chronology of Greek mythological events became increasing important to me as the list of novellas planned for this series grew to thirteen.

I have therefore prepared a simple chronology (that may or may not be consistent with other writers of this genre) to assist readers in sorting out the sequence of events that occur in the stories that I am sharing with you. (Spoiler alert!)

I now believe that Greek Mythology Chronology should be a legitimised field of study all on its own. (Perhaps it already is?)

<u>The novella.</u>	<u>The details of the event.</u>
Pisces	Gaia forms the earth, oceans and skies. She is the earth mother.
Pisces	Gaia gives birth to Uranus.
Pisces	Cronus is born and defeats Uranus when he is released from confinement.
Pisces	Aphrodite is born.
Capricorn	Pricus is the father of the sea-goats.
Pisces	Cronus is crowned king and marries Rea. Zeus is one of their six children.
Centaurus	Cronus mates with Philyra. Chiron is born.
Pandora	Prometheus creates a race of human men - It is known as the golden age.
Pisces	Zeus defeats Cronus and Zeus is crowned King of the Gods.
Pisces	Zeus marries Metis, Athena is born, but Metis dies.

Pandora   Prometheus creates a second race of human men -
              It is known as the silver age.
Pandora   Prometheus creates a third race of human men -
              It is known as the bronze age.
Pisces   Zeus marries but then quickly divorces Themis.
Pandora   Prometheus creates a fourth race of human men -
              It is known as the iron age.
Sagittarius   Crotus invents the bow and arrow.
Pisces   Zeus marries Hera. Ares, Eileithyia,
              Hephaestus, and Hebe are born.
Pisces   Aphrodite arrives at Mount Olympus
              and marries Hephaestus.
Pandora   Hephaestus creates Pandora
              as the first human woman.
Taurus   Zeus meets Europa.
Scorpio   Zeus mates with Leto and
              Apollo and Artemis are born.
Scorpio   Poseidon mates with Euryale and
              Orion is born.
Scorpio   Atalanta is recused as an infant and
              she now runs with Artemis
Aries   Zeus creates a cloud nymph named Nephele.
Aries   Poseidon mates with Theophane and
              Chrysomallos is born.
Aries   Nephele marries Athamas and
              Helle and Phrixus are born.
Aries   Chrysomallos rescues Helle and Phrixus.
Ophiuchus   Apollo mates with Coronis and
              Asclepius is born.
Cancer/Leo   Zeus mates with Alkmene and
              Herakles is born.
Gemini   Zeus mates with Leda and
              Polydeuces and Castor are born.
Pisces   Aphrodite mates with Ares. Eros is born.

Scorpio	Orion meets and befriends Hephaistos.
Virgo/Libra	Zeus visits Themis and Astraea.
Cancer/Leo	Herakles is assigned the first of his ten labours.
Cancer/Leo	Herakles befriends Chiron.
Centaurus	Chiron befriends Herakles.
Gemini	Castor and Polydeuces join the Argo crew
Cancer/Leo	Herakles joins Argo crew.
Gemini	Atalanta asks to join Argo crew.
Scorpio	Orion meets Artemis.
Centaurus	Chiron commences as a teacher.
Gemini	Herakles is inadvertently separated from the Argo.
Cancer/Leo	Herakles resumes his labours.
Scorpio	Orion duels with the giant scorpion.
Gemini	Jason and Argo crew return with the Golden Fleece.
Gemini	Calydonian Boar Hunt.
Gemini	Atalanta joins the Calydonian Boar Hunt
Cancer/Leo	Herakles accidentally wounds Chiron
Centaurus	Chiron makes his plea to Zeus.
Pisces	The Greeks and the Trojans start a war that lasts ten years.
Aquarius	Zeus meets Ganymede.
Cancer/Leo	Herakles becomes immortal and marries Hebe.
Pisces	Atalanta competes in a running race against her potential suitors.
Gemini	Castor and Polydeuces become immortal.
Pisces	Aphrodite an Eros escape Typhon.

1

The story of Ganymede the Water Bearer

The lean, tall, dark-complexioned man walked purposefully past a group of labourers. He did not glance at them. He sternly avoided their curious stares, and he kept his eyes trained on the well beaten path that stretched out before him. The workers that were constructing a fence by the path stopped to watch the stranger walk hurriedly past them. He was a welcoming distraction to them as he was dressed in unusual, but otherwise unremarkable clothing. His skin tone indicated to them that he was not a local. The overseer grunted his disapproval at the distraction, and the workers immediately resumed their toil. He shifted his position to better continue watching the foreigner as he moved steadfastly away from them. He had observed that the man was carrying a baby basket on his back. A baby seemed unlikely for a single man as they were usually in the company of the baby's mother when travelling in this fashion. But sometimes people use a baby basket to disguise the fact that they carried valuable items, such as weapons, or even precious metals and gems.

As the outsider shrunk from his view, the overseer dismissed the nefarious idea that had been forming in his greedy mind. The man was probably only carrying a change of clothing. As the stranger faded into the distance, the overseer looked about his workers and barked some more orders, urging them to complete their assigned tasks before sunset. He was becoming tired and hungry, and he now desperately wanted to return to his home.

The stranger did his utmost to appear dull and uninteresting to those people he passed. He desired only to complete his mission and return home. He had been travelling by foot for the past eleven days, having arrived by boat on the eastern shore of this land. He was far from home and whilst he spoke the Greek languages, he knew that he stood out among the common people. As he was ordered to do so, he always headed farther inland in a generally westerly direction.

He was carrying some food and clothing for the baby, and he responsibly attended to its needs. He had sufficient local coins to buy more food for both of them, and he never bought more than he could carry. He was a married man and a father himself and so he was experienced with baby's demands. He, and his wife that he loved deeply, both loved and cared for their children. But this baby boy was not his. He did not even know who the baby's parents were, and whilst he had some notion about their importance, he reasoned that knowing the truth, or even daring to speculate about it, may led to him having an insecure future. He would be paid handsomely for discreetly relocating the child, and then he was required to forget that it had ever happened. He and his family would be safe. These were good enough reasons for him to accomplish this mission. When this task was completed, he would return home to his wife and children and forget all about this baby.

The baby started to complain. It was becoming increasingly restless in the basket behind him. As the man was walking, he was searching for a suitable camp for the night. Generally, he ventured off the main roads and pathways to hide in a dense grove of trees, or if possible, he would venture off to be behind a mound or small hill. When they passed a stream, he would refill his canteens and if the location provided sufficient privacy, he would bath both himself and his small charge.

He preferred to be alone with the baby. His knowledge of the local Greek language was sufficient to get by, but whenever he was in company of locals, it usually involved having a conversation. This inevitably meant that curious people start asking awkward questions which he did not want to answer. Regardless of how respectful for his privacy they had intended to be, he knew his disposition stimulated their intrigue. He did not want that, so he did his best to avoid the company of other travellers.

The fields were covered in lush green grasses, and he judged that this land was fertile, and that the vegetation was sustained with ample rainfall. There were a wide variety of fruits and vegetable crops for him to harvest and feed himself. He occasionally brought down a rabbit with his sling shot. He also had a hunting knife which he carefully secreted in his clothing as any visible weapons often attracted the wrong type of attention. He wished he had his bow and arrows. With them, they would eat better, but these weapons would be visible and would result in officious demands for explanations from the administrators and their enforcers of these lands he passed through. They would insist on knowing his true purpose for being here.

The farther up the mountains the man and the baby travelled, the more sheep he saw. He was comfortable with the sheep and their attending shepherds. His own family were shepherds, and although he had not chosen that life for himself, he was raised as a child to one day become one.

They came upon a small structure and he immediately recognised its purpose. It was slightly different from those built on his family's sheep grazing lands, but he knew it would function in the same way.

It was a crude shelter that one or two shepherds would use to quarter themselves when they were too far from the home to return before night-time.

From experience the man hoped that he would find a soft sheep-skin to sleep on. There should be a water source close by and possibly even some dried food supplies that had been securely stored. He walked up the grassy slope and into the shelter, and he was relieved to find it empty of humans. He and the baby settled in for the night.

His first task was to feed, clean, and re-clothe the baby. He did so and thought to himself how little fuss this child had caused him. He knew from his own personal experience that this placid behaviour was rare. His own children were bawling, demanding, and always hungry. This baby seemed happy by nature and was easily contented. He smiled when receiving the administrations of the man, and he slept peacefully enough when he was fed, cleaned, and dressed in fresh clothing. This baby had adapted to the changing circumstances as best as the man could hope for. The baby watched him has he attended to his own eating and cleaning needs. He then gently rocked the child and soon the baby was asleep. Feeling tired from the journey, he too was soon dreaming of being reunited with his loved one's.

The following dawn he woke to the sounds of deep snoring. He looked about him and noticed that a large bearish man was sound asleep in the shelter with them. He had not heard him come in and he had clearly settled himself in for the night without expressing any concern about him or the baby as intruders. Maybe having a baby sig-nified to the shepherd that he was a humble family man and not a warrior or thief. The man thought through the rationale and con-cluded that this was highly likely.

His own childhood as a shepherd was a difficult one, but he was loved and nurtured by his family, and he was always kept busy with managing the flock. He learned many skills that gave him advantages over the other men he had served with. He examined the sleeping hulk of the man and he quickly came to a decision. The baby would be safe with these people and the baby boy would remain anonymous living here. He decided to leave the baby with this shepherd and he immediately commence his journey homeward.

With the decision made, the man quietly stood up. He looked at the baby who stared back at him. The baby smiled at him and he was gratified with the baby's confidence in him. He also decided that the baby was agreeing as if in some acquiescence to the man's decision to leave him in the care of shepherds.

He left the shelter to the sounds of snoring resonating behind him. When he reached the road, he turned east, hastily retracing his route towards the coast and embark on his ship-bound journey to his home-land.

Moments later, his travelling companion now departed, the hungry baby cried for food. The man stirred and quickly attended the baby. At first, he was confused, and was hopeful that the stranger would return to his child, but slowly he realised that this baby had been deserted. The baby seemed contented and healthy. He could not figure out why he had been forsaken and he knew that he could not abandon the child to the elements. So, he happily decided to take him home and submit him into his family's care. He hoped his wife will be delighted with a new addition to their family. They would teach the boy to become one of them.

The shepherd returned home to his wife and children, and the nine other families that shared the land and worked the sheep. They all agreed to adopt the baby and that he would make a fine addition to their little group. Together, they would raise him and teach him the skills he would need to become a great shepherd.

Someone commented that the baby seemed completely aware of what was happening, and that he appeared to accept them all remarkably well. The shepherd's wife suggested that they name him Ganymede because of his happy disposition. He seemed to brighten up the room and was quite happy to be with them. As no one had a different suggestion, that name, quite unceremoniously, became his.

***

So, Ganymede was adopted by the family of the shepherd that found himself awake next to an abandoned baby. His new mother immediately fell in love with the baby and he fitted into their domestic routine as comfortably as if she herself had given birth to him. His growth rate was normal, he was exceptionally healthy, and as a toddler his physical activity skills meant that he could soon keep up with the other children. He eagerly participated in all manner of play and exercise. But it was his problem-solving skills that impressed everyone, and he was making worthwhile suggestions and observations as soon as he could speak sentences. When he spoke, he had a ready audience as they enjoyed his company and were generally supportive of what he had to contribute. He ate appreciatively, but never greedily, and he mostly cooperated and did as he was bid, unless he could suggest a better way. He was polite, respectful, dutiful, and loyal. His adopted siblings, and the children of the other families approved of him and he was treated by everyone as one of their own. He suffered no cruelty, bullying, or unnecessary hardship, and he seemed to the villagers that he was a cheerful and well-adjusted child.

Ganymede commenced his training on how to manage sheep as soon as he could walk. By the time he was eight years old, he had two sheep dogs that loved and obeyed him. The three of them could round up and pen a significant sized mob of sheep. When asked to do so, he and his dogs relocated the sheep so that they would eat from different pastures, as sheep will overgraze on the grass shoots if left to do so on their own determination. He ensured that they visited the watering points often enough, and he kept them from straying off. He and his dogs watched out for poachers and for predators.

One day, a giant eagle circled the skies above his flock. His mature sheep were too large and bulky with fleece to present an opportunity for the eagle, even one as large as this. Still, Ganymede was wary and watchful. The eagle might be hungry enough to attempt to try and take one, and this would panic the flock, scattering them in all directions. Their fleeing would result in a huge workload for him and the dogs.

The eagle swooped lower, now looking for an opportunity to pluck out a smaller, weaker sheep, from the flock that it would try to carry away to kill and eat. Ganymede shouted at it, and he frantically waved his arms in a futile attempt to dissuade the giant bird. The eagle gathered height momentarily, but it soon commenced its dive and swooped, seemingly determined that it will catch food here. The dogs barked noisily at the eagle, determined to warn the giant bird to stay away. But the dogs were also wary of this predator as they might become its prey also. Ganymede took off his knitted top and waved it about in the air above his head. He wanted the eagle to believe that he was taller and stronger than he actually was, in the hope that it would urge the bird to break away from pouncing on one of his sheep. The eagle saw Ganymede's charge and it now changed its mind and broke away from its swooping attack. It flapped its enormous wings, and with a shriek of contempt, flew away in search of an easier meal in a different region.

Ganymede later pondered his encounter with the eagle. It was only when the eagle thought that he was a man, that it gave up its attack. Ganymede decided that he needed to appear taller. He fashioned a head, torso, and arms from dried grass, lengths of cut branches, and bound it together with vines. He dressed it in some old clothing. He then held the top half of the manly shaped figurine as high as he could. From a distance, he now appeared much taller than he actually was. But his masterpiece was both heavy and fragile and it would become tiresome to carry it around with him. He concluded that it might work in an emergency, but otherwise it was not a practical defence against a determined predator.

Ganymede awoke one morning with a new idea for intimidating predators. He set off and constructed several adult sized human replicas from branches and cut grass. He dressed them in discarded clothing and positioned them across the hill side paddocks that he mostly managed. The sheep and his dogs ignored them, but for a while it seemed to keep the wolves and eagles away.

At first the shepherds laughed at him and ridiculed his fake family. But they soon realised the cleverness of his idea, and soon they were also making fake shepherds for their other paddocks. The following lambing season was their most successful ever, as they lost the fewest number of lambs to the persistent carnivorous beasts than in any previous lambing season. Some old sheep were sacrificed and prepared for cooking on spits above a large open fire. A feast was prepared especially to honour Ganymede and celebrate this young man's initiative.

***

By the time Ganymede was fifteen years old, he had grown to his full adult height. He was tall but still gangling, as he had yet to bulk out into a mature manly figure. Despite his leanness, Ganymede was an outstandingly handsome young man. He was lithe, muscular, and athletic. His boyish face was unblemished, and with his olive skin he generally radiated happiness sporting a healthy complexion. His naturally long curly jet-black hair was the envy of some of the women, and a few of the girls about his age were now noticing him in a positive romantic way. Each was hoping that he might one day give one of them some intimate attention. But Ganymede remained polite, friendly, and he was certainly helpful, but he was not attentive toward any of the young women who wanted him in that way. This was despite their increasingly overt and somewhat desperate attempts to use their emerging feminine charms on him.

It seemed to the others that Ganymede was focused on his chores and caring for the sheep, and he would not be distracted by girlish whims as easily as the other boys were. The elders were delighted to discreetly observe these harmless interactions with some mirthful interest, as they all hoped that someday, when Ganymede was older and more experienced, that he would marry for love and raise his own family.

***

After the drowning of a lamb caught unawares in the fast-flowing river, Ganymede excavated a channel along the river's edge to allow the sheep to drink from calmer waters. Encouraged by his elders, he next devised several channels that redirected the flowing water to where the crops were being grown, thus saving many hours of toil bringing water to the crops by bucket. He next organised the excavation a medium sized earth dam that was filled by diverting some of the rivers fast flowing winter rains. When finished, it held more than enough water to last them during the drier summer months.

Their sheep flourished and their food reserves were never low. The sale of surplus sheep and crops to the local villages and merchants, allowed them to purchase comforts such as cloth and exotic foods. Ganymede was loved and respected by his family and he felt safe and happy.

One fine summer's day, with the assistance of his two old dogs, he moved a large flock of mature sheep to an upper field. The three rested whilst looking over their charges. The dogs were still panting from their exertion, and they came to him for pats and cuddles, which he affectionately gave them. They rested in the shade watching the sheep contentedly grazing on the long grass when Ganymede and the dogs heard a rustling in the trees behind them. The dogs began to growl in warning and they turned toward Ganymede for his instructions. All three were now peering in the trees and bushes to see if any threat emerged. The noise stopped and they slowly began to relax again, but they continued to glance in the direction where they thought the sounds had come from.

Moments later, after a burst of loud noise, an unusual looking creature emerged from the bush. It stood still, as if measuring them. The dogs whimpered and were clearly uncertain of what to do. They both watched Ganymede for orders, but he held them back, now fearful this creature may do harm to the dogs if he ordered them to attack.

The beast made a gesture with his hand and the dogs crouched closer to the ground. Ganymede regarded his dogs with concern, but was surprised to discover that both his companions were sound asleep and rendered unable to assist him.

'Hello, Ganymede,' the creature spoke to him in gentle tones.

'Hello,' Ganymede replied cautiously. He was puzzled about how the creature knew his name.

The creature now moved farther out into the open. The top half of the beast seemed human in appearance except for two protruding bone like horns that appeared above is scalp hair. However, the bottom half of the creature was more like the hind shaggy legs of a goat, with hooves instead of feet.

'Do you know who I am?' the creature asked.

'Yes,' Ganymede answered uncertain of how this encounter will proceed. 'You are "Pan", God of all the shepherds.'

'Good,' he replied as he considered the young man. 'Are you frightened?' he asked showing mild concern.

'Just a little. But I am also honoured that you would choose to speak with me,' Ganymede answered him.

'What a charming man,' Pan concluded as he stepped closer.

Ganymede said nothing and stood his ground.

'Many people panic when they see me. Even the word panic evolved from my name, which is funny because I am a god of fertility, and I even compose and play delightful music.'

'It might be because of your unusual appearance,' Ganymede suggested.

Pan smiled benevolently. 'You won't know this, but I have been discreetly observing you for a long time now. You are an excellent shepherd, Ganymede.' he explained as if it were a statement of fact.

'Thank you for the compliment.' Ganymede responded. 'But why are you interested in me?'

'I know that you were not born for this life,' Pan continued.

'I think I was,' contradicted Ganymede.

'No, you weren't.'

Ganymede sat still and said nothing. The dogs were still sleeping and Ganymede could hear their noisy breathing. It sounded reassuring that they were okay.

'Maybe one day you will learn about your past and how you came to be living here,' Pan advised him. 'Or maybe you won't.'

'It does not matter,' Ganymede told him. 'This is my life and these people are my family,' he gestured down the valley.

'Good for you!' Pan exclaimed. 'However, I am here to explain to you that you can have a different future to this shepherd's life you are currently envisaging.'

'I do not understand.'

'I know that.'

'What will become of me?'

'I know that many things will happen to you, and that you will one day have to make major determinations about your future. They will be significant and far-reaching decisions. Your fate is still being decided... and that mostly, your options will be chosen by you,' Pan explained. He nodded as he smiled at him. It was a kindly knowing smile.

Ganymede said nothing. His father's teachings of one day becoming the master of his own fate resonated in his mind, but he had always envisaged a future here as a shepherd living a sheepherder's life. Pan was a god and the gods knew about these things, so he listened intently.

'It is important that you know, that wherever your path takes you, that these people that you have called your family will continue to be safe, happy, and they will all continue to thrive without you.'

'Am I going to die?'

Pan laughed. 'All mortals die! It takes much longer for us Gods to cease to exist than it does for you humans, but all of us succumb in the end!'

'So, you are not planning to kill me?'

'Kill you!?' Pan burst out into laughter. 'No dear Ganymede. You should live for an exceptionally long time. It is how well you prosper while living your life that will be mostly up to you.'

Ganymede looked at him pensively.

Pan continued, 'When you leave here, my forest nymphs and I will watch over your extended family and their sheep. I implore you not to worry about them.'

'When am I leaving? Why should I want to? I don't understand. Can I say farewell to them before I leave?'

'When the time comes, you will know what to do,' Pan advised him. 'Goodbye Ganymede, we will meet again.' Pan turned and headed back into the bush from wherever he came from.

Ganymede stared in that direction, but could not see or hear him anymore. The dog's stirred and he crouched low to check on them. They whimpered and came to him licking his face apologetically for falling asleep on the job. He hugged them both and they wagged their tails fiercely in loving appreciation.

For a while, Ganymede remained alert for any life altering events, but as the days and weeks passed, his life was about the routine of caring and tending to the flock. He slowly put aside Pan's words, and he focused on just being a good shepherd.

***

Time passed as time does. The summers came and went. The routine for Ganymede now seemed to be set in stone. He tended the flocks, solved watering issues, attended the crops with the women, ate, drank, slept, washed and did it day in and day out. He and his friends played, walked, and talked, and it was nearly always about the sheep.

He like to swim in the dam and he was often accompanied by the others in his age group. They splashed each other and frolicked happily with the dog's barking encouragement.

One day his father and brother approached him as he relaxed in the summer sun chewing on sour weed. He had always known that these were not his natural father and brother, but it made no difference to him or to them. His adopted father's wife was also his mother and they shared a modest home that was constructed of branches, straw, sticks, and mud. It was a simple life and he was proud to be a part of their family.

'Ganymede.'

'Yes father.'

'Your brother is marrying.'

Ganymede was ecstatic. He leapt up and hugged his brother Amos affectionately.

They were about two years apart in age, and Amos had done a commendable job of tolerating Ganymede as his younger, more intelligent, adopted brother. Their rivalry had only ever been playful and Amos had mostly shown concern for Ganymede's well-being, but Ganymede had little need to be "looked after".

'It is Astrid, isn't it?'

'Yes,' Amos replied as he blushed.

'Astrid will make a man out of you son,' their father declared proudly patting him on the back.

Amos said nothing, but he appeared daunted by the future responsibility of becoming a husband.

Ganymede smiled.

'Now, Ganymede,' started his father. 'You know that Astrid has a younger sister.'

'Beth,' replied Ganymede knowingly.

'Her father and I have observed the two of you swimming and you seem to be spending much time together.'

Ganymede looked concerned about where this conversation was heading. 'It is more that she likes spending time with me. I just let her do so to keep her happy.'

Amos appeared as if he were about to burst into laughter. The smile on his face was enormous. 'I have observed her preparing gifts for you,' he explained. 'She truly loves you,' he added teasingly.

Ganymede blushed, but his olive complexion hid it well.

'Beth's father and I agree that you are both the right age to marry also,' his father declared. 'You two will make a good match,' his father concluded.

Amos could contain himself no longer and he burst out into laughter.

Their father gave him a reproachful glare, and so Amos took in a deep breath and settled.

'But...'

'No but's son...' his father interrupted. 'Your mother and Beth's mother are already adding your wedding needs to Amos's and Astrid's wedding preparations. The whole community is a buzz.'

'But...' Ganymede tried vainly to object.

Amos sniggered some more. 'Oh, there will be plenty of butt brother!' he laughed once more at his own joke.

'But, father!' Ganymede appealed. 'I'm only nineteen!' he exclaimed.

'And so is Beth!' his father retorted. 'It is time she had a baby in her belly.'

Amos again burst into laughter. Ganymede gave him the "you are so immature" look.

Amos stared deeply into Ganymede's face. 'Come on brother, you have watched rams tup ewes often enough. You know what you have to do,' he explained smiling benevolently.

Ganymede's face turned ashen. He did not feel ready for this.

'It is time that both of you left our nest and gave your mother and I some privacy. We will soon start work on building a new home for each of you, and they will be completed for you to move into by your wedding day!' promised their father.

Ganymede was devastated.

His father went off to share the joyous news with the other villagers. Amos stayed with his younger brother. He had suddenly become quiet and sullen.

Ganymede looked at Amos and spoke softly. 'I am still a virgin,' he confided.

'So am I,' Amos declared. 'And I am two years older than you.' His face flushed.

'But...'

'So far, no butt,' he explained sniggering. 'Just my trusty hand,' he held it up and waved it about.

'Me too,' confessed Ganymede.

'Up in the shelter in the top paddock?'

'Yes.'

'Me too.'

'Oh.' Ganymede looked down.

'I think all of us have done that up there,' Amos added.

'Oh,' Ganymede replied and looked up.

They were both quiet for a moment.

'Have you ever…' Ganymede began to ask.

'With an ewe?' Amos was horrified. 'No! Never.'

'Me neither,' agreed Ganymede.

'I think one of the others tried to do it once.'

'Who was it?'

'I shouldn't tell.'

'Did it work?'

'He would not say.'

'Oh.'

They were both silent for a bit.

'So, with a woman then,' Amos added as if needing something to say.

'I guess,' agreed Ganymede.

'Let us hope that we do not embarrass ourselves. We would never hear the end of it from father if we did,' Amos cautioned him.

'That is so true,' Ganymede conceded. 'Have you ever asked him about it?'

'What? Doing it with a woman?'

'Yes.'

'I never thought to do so. I guess everyone here learns about it from watching the rams and the dogs...'

'I have heard father and mother... you know...' Ganymede explained hesitatingly.

Amos stood up seemingly embarrassed. He turned and left Ganymede sitting on the grass. He hastily walked away without saying any more.

It suddenly occurred to Ganymede that this was probably the weirdest conversation that he had ever had with his older brother. He was inwardly pleased that they had shared so much.

***

The following day, Ganymede was with a flock of sheep near the watering station that he had previously designed and constructed. He sat with his dogs watching the sheep as they drank from the calm, cool, clean water. He heard a noise behind him and he and the dogs looked up to see Beth approaching them. The dogs rose up, tails wagging and walked up to her to offer her their affection. Ganymede stood awkwardly.

She squatted briefly and patted and hugged the dogs with loving familiarity. Then smilingly she stood up and came over to Ganymede.

'I feel that I should kiss and hug you, since we are destined to be married,' she said to him wide-eyed.

Uncertain and shyly, he leaned forward to her and they embraced. They had often wrestled as children. Touching and holding each other was not awkward, it was natural. But now, as they had been told they had been promised to each other in marriage, it felt weird.

'Beth...' He began to vocalise his misgivings.

'Ganymede,' she replied, smiling at his awkwardness. She reached up and put one hand on his face.

'You know I like you,' he explained speaking down to the ground. 'I like you a lot...'

'We have been friends all our lives,' she confirmed.

'Good friends,' he agreed, looking up at her.

'I had always hoped that one day we would become... you know,' she seemed to be more confident than he felt.

'Married?'

'Yes!' she smiled broadly. Her eyes widened.

'Oh,' he muttered and looked down again.

'And you know… intimate.' She withheld a girlish giggle.

He blushed, but said nothing.

'Are you shy, Ganymede?' she asked, her smile was captivating and she seemed pleased at the effect this was having on her intended.

'Well, it is just that…' he hesitated, unsure of how to explain himself.

'We have seen each other naked before,' she observed.

'Yes, exactly! But we have never… you know.'

'Shared our bodies for sex,' she stated maturely, 'Is that what you are trying to say to me, Ganymede?'

'Well, yes. We have never even talked about that possibility.'

'I should think not,' she confirmed. 'I was always planning that our first time should be special and wonderfully romantic.'

'I see,' he said as he drew in a deep breath. He was feeling awkward about this revelation as he had never even imagined it.

'It is not that I haven't thought about doing it with you, because I sure have, lots of times,' she studied him for his reaction hoping it would be mutual.

Ganymede said nothing. Her smile was warm and inviting, and he sensed that she wanted to be kissed.

'Each time our naked bodies touched, my pangs of longing for you grew wilder. I could hardly keep my hands away from touching you down there,' she explained as she was looking down at his groin region. 'But we didn't, and we haven't, but soon we will be married and then we can be totally free to love and pleasure each other whenever we choose.'

Ganymede turned pale. Again, his olive complexion hid his response.

Beth continued. 'The benefit of having an older sister is that she has told me a lot of what to expect,' she explained.

'I thought she was a...' Ganymede's voice trailed off. 'He then remembered that Beth and Astrid had a much older sister and that she was already married.

'What is wrong, Ganymede?' Beth asked concerned.

'I am not sure?'

'Not sure about what?' she demanded.

'About everything,' he mumbled.

'How do you mean?' she was clearly confused and becoming upset.

'About us... about rushing into marriage,' he explained looking directly into her face. 'We are still so young....' He was relieved to finally verbalise his misgivings, as he knew deep down that he had an obligation to explain them to her. He was also aware that he had deeply disappointed her. He wanted to look away, to change the subject, to run and hide in the hills, be struck by lightning, be taken by a wolf, anything.

'Oh,' she responded looking down.

Ganymede looked at his feet, willing them to run.

'So, you think we are rushing into marriage,' she concluded. 'I will tell my parents that you need more time to get used to the idea of becoming my husband. They will understand.'
Ganymede said nothing.

'We will work on our courtship together. We can prepare for marriage at a later date.'

Ganymede still said nothing.

'Girls always mature faster than boys,' she concluded. 'I can wait until you are ready,' she concluded and smiled lovingly toward him.

Beth was always so clever, organised, and determined. Ganymede knew that she would make someone a great wife, be a devoted mother, and possibly even a dutiful lover. He just believed that he was not the man for her. She was kind, clever, skilled in womanly tasks and he should feel honoured that she wanted him, but he didn't and he did not understand why that was so.

She touched his arm and he looked up into her face. She gave him a gentle smile and turned to walk back home.

Ganymede watched her go. The dogs followed her for a bit, hoping for another pat, but she ignored them. He slumped and sat heavily on the ground. He glanced at the sheep as his eyes welled with tears. The dogs sensing that something was wrong, nuzzled their way up from under his arms to lick his face. He smiled at their faithful attempt to cheer him up.

***

When Ganymede returned with the sheep, he penned them securely. He fed the dogs and washed before entering his parent's house.

'There you are son,' his father greeted him.

His mother and brother watched and listened in silence.

'I have had a visit from Beth's father.'

Ganymede said nothing. He nodded and looked at him as if willing him to continue.

'So, you think we are rushing you into marriage.'

Ganymede still said nothing but he managed to nod imperceptibly.

'Weddings take a lot of preparation son,' his father began by way of an explanation.

Ganymede stood in silence and listened patiently. From experience he knew it was better not to interrupt, speak, or even give a visual clue of agreement or disagreement, as his father would leap at it as either confirmation or confrontation of whatever it was that he was saying.

'The more couples that get hitched at a single event, the easier it is for all the families involved to arrange it and to pay for it,' he explained.

Ganymede stood still, his features emotionless.

His father continued, 'That way we can all have a good time, without it severely draining our resources.'

Ganymede understood that this was true. He had been to several wedding celebrations before, just not his own.

'Why are you being awkward about this, son? Don't you fancy Beth?'

Ganymede hesitated answering. He had formulated an idea of how to deal with this situation but had not yet formed the words.

Then he blurted, 'I just wish that it could have been my idea,' he stated. 'I am being told that I am suitable to be married to Beth, but no one has ever asked me if I love her, or if I want to be married to her!'

His father was able to remain patient and calm. 'Arranged marriages are quite normal. As we are your parents, we get to decide what is best for you. At least you already know that Beth loves you. I had not even met your mother before we became betrothed, as she came to me from a neighbouring community. We married, then fell in love, and now we are happy.'

He turned to face his mother and she nodded her agreement.

'On our wedding day, it was only the fourth time that I had met him,' she confirmed.

'Beth is such an agreeable girl,' his father continued, intent on promoting the arrangement to Ganymede. 'She is also attractive, so that is a bonus. You will be lucky to have her, and if you wait too long someone else will snap her up.'

'You do not want a life filled with regrets,' his mother cautioned.

'You know what they say, "hesitate, or procrastinate, and you will inwardly remonstrate",' his father explained and he clearly enjoyed sharing his wisdom.

'Her mother assures me that she is an adequate cook and she improves as she learns to prepare different meals. She will work tirelessly, and she will always keep your home clean and organised,' added his mother.

'And I will bet that she will be a real goer in bed,' Amos said his eyes now wide open with mischief.

Their parents glared at Amos disapprovingly.

Ganymede sighed as Amos shrugged it off, but he winked at Ganymede conspiratorially.

Their father took in a deep breath. 'Look son, why don't you take the dogs and a flock of sheep up to the high paddock for a couple of days? I had thought that you would happily want to marry Beth, but clearly this a difficult decision for you, and so I now think you should have some quiet time to ponder what is best for you.'

Ganymede nodded his agreement. Some time away from this craziness would be good for him.

'Beth is certainly a great girl, and whilst we are confident that you will be good together...' his father assured him while turning toward his wife for affirmation and she nodded her agreement. '... and I am sure, that in just a short time, after you get used to the idea, that you will understand and agree just how lucky you are.' He was now studying Ganymede, waiting for him to positively respond.

But Ganymede simply nodded his acquiescence.

'Enough said!' his father confirmed looking at the others who also nodded their agreement.

The conversation was concluded. His parents hugged him and Amos punched his arm.

They ate, talked about sheep, the dogs, the weather, anything but marriage. His mother assured him that she would pack some food for him to take to the top paddock and reminded him that he should take warm clothing with him as it was starting to get cooler in the evenings.

He embraced her and promised that he intended to do so.

***

The following morning, Ganymede took his two favourite dogs, and a large flock of sheep, and they headed up the hill to the high paddock. It took most of the day to get there as parts of the climb were quite steep and he needed to rest the sheep and the dogs and complete the journey in stages. As well as clothing and food for him, he also carried four large water bladders as he believed there would not yet be enough clean water in the winter ponds despite recent rains.

Ganymede had a difficult night. Total darkness was a sheepherder's friend, but on this evening, there were clear skies and a full moon. It was always more challenging to sleep in the high country as he was often alone, and any required assistance was too far away to summon. He and the dogs had heard signs of wildlife in the forest and he was anxious for the safety of the flock. During a moonlit night, mountain lions, foxes, and wolves, were more audacious in the pursuit of catching and killing a young sheep. He and the dogs spent the first part of the evening on high alert for predators. Later, drowsy with exhaustion, he had succumbed to a restless sleep.

At sunrise, Ganymede and the dogs walked the field. He counted the sheep and was relieved that they were all present and were contentedly chewing on the damp grass, still wet from the heavy morning dew. They will get most of their moisture requirements directly from the wet grass. He and the dogs however needed a drink from the water bladders. He fed the dogs and poured water into a bowl for them. After a feed of bread, dried meat, and an apple, he next checked the shelter for obvious damage. When he was satisfied that everything was intact, he checked the ponds. Each had a muddy puddle at the bottom and he knew that it would take some heavy autumn rains to fill them back up.

Later in the day, Ganymede set some rabbit traps for food for the dogs and himself. He then basked in the sunshine and contentedly watched the sheep as they constantly jostled for position for the greenest juiciest grass. He suddenly appreciated his life and began thinking that maybe he should spend more of his time in the high country.

He thought of the times he had spent alone in this shelter in the high paddock. It was a good place and he enjoyed the freedom to think, uninterrupted by well-meaning family and friends who persistently wanted to know what he was doing. The view was spectacular. It was filled with mountain peaks, forests of trees whose leaves were now starting to show rich autumn colours, and deep in the valley he could sometimes see sunlight reflected off the flowing river. Also, you could see people approaching from a long way off, but visitors were rare. The forest behind the shelter offered abundant firewood which he collected and stacked in readiness for cooking his meal and for the comfort and warmth that a campfire provided. Later, he would check the rabbit traps. He was confident of a cooked rabbit meal tonight, as his traps had never failed him.

Ganymede entered the shelter intending to rest. He thought about his dilemma with Beth. How could he tell is best friend that he does love her, but not as a man loves a woman, but more as how a brother loves his favourite sister.

He sat relaxed on the make shift bed under the roof of the shelter resting his eyes. He reached under his clothing and tugged on his loins. He continued thinking about Beth. He had seen her naked enough times to be able to imagine her lying naked on a bed wanting him to enter her, but for some reason it did nothing to arouse him. He always knew that he only liked her as a friend, but never as a potential lover. He was confused as he was supposed to get aroused by the thoughts of being naked with a woman. His father and brother seemed to get immense pleasure from it. He then realised that he had never felt that way about any girl or woman, not that he had met many of them.

His thoughts drifted and they were now about the conversation he had had with Amos, and he thought about the generations of young males who had lain where he now lay, away from the ever-watchful eyes of family and the other villagers, being able to do what he was now doing, satisfying sexual urges in complete privacy.

This was a delightful thought and the effect was almost instantaneous. The image in his mind of other males pleasuring themselves had granted him his desired arousal. His member grew erect and hard. He stood up and shed his clothing and he examined his engorged penis lovingly. He continued long tugs and strokes, manipulating the shaft and thus delaying the pleasure and the ultimate ecstasy of ejaculation.

He continued this way for some time, enjoying the liberation of privacy when suddenly he heard movement from outside which startled him. He had believed he was alone. At first, he thought that maybe Beth had climbed the hill to be with him, but then he discounted that conclusion as it was too far and he did not believe that she would find her way to the high mountain shelter. He looked at the two dogs who huddled together on an old blanket. They continued to sleep soundlessly. He slowed his ministrations to just enough to keep it erect when a large old ewe casually walked into his shelter.

'Go away!' he yelled at the ewe.

The dogs awoke and quickly ran to his aid. They did not seem to mind the ewe's presence and they clearly did not understand it as a threat to Ganymede. They both looked about unsure of what to do. One attempted to lick Ganymede's face in reassurance, but he pushed the dog off his bed.

'Just great,' he stood up with his still erect phallus waving about in front of him. 'Get out, all of you.'

The dogs retreated to the doorway looking at him confused and worried, but the ewe just stood its ground staring up at him.

Ganymede sat back down on the bed. He wondered if this ewe was a previous participant in the other boy's sheep shagging. Do the ewes enjoy it? Do they desire human penetration? Had it known and entered the shelter in anticipation of being desired by him? Ganymede sighed. No, he thought. That was ridiculous reasoning. It was only a weird coincidence that the ewe was present when he was pleasuring himself, and he had felt no desire to fornicate with it.

The old ewe just stood still, looking at him, not moving. He sighed and decided to return his attention to his ejaculation. He was so close and so he lay back down and he turned to face away from the sheep as it was distracting him.

He was just about to explode when the sheep bleated. He stopped and sighed. He must get rid of this ewe and shut the door to get some privacy. He rose from his bed and grabbed the sheep, forcibly turning its head toward the door. The ewe was large and cumbersome, and he had to position himself behind it in order to heave it outside, when he heard a person enter the hut. He looked up to see that it was Beth. She was horrified seeing Ganymede with his erection waving in the air and a sheep's rear end before him. She was clearly distressed by what she had witnessed, and she immediately turned around and walked back outside, tears forming.

Ganymede abandoned his efforts in evicting the ewe and ran after her.

'Keep that thing away from me,' she warned him.

His "thing" was shrinking fast. 'Beth...'

'I came here to tell you how much I love you and prove to you that I wanted you,' she wailed. 'But no! You prefer sheep! You are a sheep shagger!' she heavily enunciated the words in accusation.

'No, I'm not!' he blurted.

'It certainly looks that way to me.'

'I was just... pleasuring myself and that sheep just came into the room by itself.'

'What!'

'It just walked in.'

'I suppose you have a name for her?'

'What?'

'Well, if she feels that comfortable just walking in, she must be a close and personal friend of yours. What name do you have for her?'

'I do not have a name for her!' he yelled. 'And I do not shag sheep!'

'And you obviously do not want to shag me either,' she stated and it was clearly rhetorical. She folded her arms and turned her back on him.

Ganymede felt deflated. 'Beth,' he implored. 'You know me. I would never harm a sheep...'

'It is okay Ganymede,' she capitulated and seemed to concede defeat. She drew in a deep breath and sighed heavily. 'At least I now understand why you do not want to marry me.'

Ganymede said nothing.

'I will explain to both our parents that you prefer sheep shagging to the real thing. They will understand why I cannot marry you, and that one day I will marry loving man who likes girls and not sheep.'

Ganymede still did not reply. He inwardly conceded that the evidence against him was compelling.

'Put some clothes on. You look cold,' she said indicating his now shrivelled member.

Ganymede blushed but nodded.

'I am going home to be with my family. You had better stay up here for a long time. I don't think you will be popular when you come back down the mountain.' She turned and left stomping noisily as she proceeded to walk downhill. His dogs stood dutifully beside him and the three watched her walk away, go over the crest of the slope, and out of view.

Humiliated, Ganymede suddenly felt cold and alone in the world, when a voice called from behind him.

'Ganymede,' the voice called.

Ganymede stared into the woods and tried to identify the voice.

The voice continued to speak. 'You are a handsome young man.'

Ganymede ran into the shelter and he immediately came back out armed with a long pointy stick and a hunting knife. He waved them about trying to appear intimidating.

The voice laughed. 'Careful, you may injure yourself.'

'Where are you?' Ganymede demanded. 'Why are you here?'

'To bring you a message,' the voice told him.

He heard the sounds of twigs snapping to his left and he turned to see a half man half goat creature looking at him.

'Pan,' Ganymede recognised him.

'Indeed, yes, it is me!' Pan giggled.

'Why, what, when?' Ganymede blurted.

'Yes, I saw it all,' Pan explained and laughed hysterically.

'But then.'

'When I saw the young woman heading up the hill, I drove that ewe into your shelter!' he laughed once more.

'You did what!' Ganymede was flabbergasted. 'Why would you do that?' he demanded.

'Oh, the expression on her face was priceless. I promise you, that I shall take her look of astonishment and disgust to my grave,' he sighed.

'You have ruined me,' Ganymede lamented now feeling resigned to his rapidly diminishing status within his community.

'No, sweet Ganymede,' Pan contradicted him. 'As this adventure ends, a better one will take its place. Remember that long ago I explained to you that you were destined for bigger and more exciting things.'

Ganymede nodded but without conviction.

'That day has come,' Pan advised him.

'How?' Ganymede wanted to understand.

'Fate.'

'Oh.'

'Now, your abandonment of this lifestyle will not cause any surprises to your family.'

'What if I do not want to leave?'

'You can stay with your family and live in disgrace and misery, or you can accept a proposal to depart from here and you will flourish.'

'Please explain your proposal?' Ganymede was now realising that he did not have much of a choice.

'Not mine, dear boy,' Pan pointed to a man that was standing before them. He was tall, muscular, heavily bearded, and Ganymede immediately thought him strikingly handsome. 'His,' Pan said as he pointed and then vanished.

'Hello Ganymede,' said the man. 'I have been looking forward to meeting you for a long time now,' the man spoke with a gentle and kindly voice. He smiled and then added, 'My name is Zeus.'

Ganymede was astonished at the realisation of the significance of the deity that was standing before him. Zeus! The King of all the gods was here... visiting him!

Zeus laughed a gentle knowing laugh. He stepped up closer to Ganymede and held his shoulders in greeting. He then turned Ganymede and gently pushed him toward the shelter. They went inside and they sat on the bed next to each other.

Ganymede said nothing. He was suddenly aware that he was still naked and seated next to the King of all the Gods. He motioned to cover his private parts with some bedding and Zeus laughed. 'Do not be embarrassed. I truly enjoy seeing you naked and I would actually prefer that you remain that way. You are an exceptionally beautiful man.'

Ganymede blushed a little and was not sure what to think. He decided to change the subject. 'How do you happen to be here?'

'I can fly...' Zeus began to explain.

'Fly?'

'Yes. As a god I have many talents. Transforming myself into an eagle is just one of them.'

'An eagle?'

'Yes. And as an eagle, I can swiftly travel long distances. I know, I appreciate that I can materialise anywhere anytime I choose, but flying gives me a much better appreciation over everything. I can encompass the situation before I land, and that gives me significant advantages.'

Ganymede said nothing. He stared at the god in awe and disbelief that he was here.

'Over the many years that I have flown over this valley, I have been watching you grow into a fine specimen of a man. Now that you are an adult, I felt it was time that I met with you in person.'

'Oh.'

'I remember flying over you when you were much younger, just a boy. I was hungry. I was in my eagle form and I swooped low over your sheep looking for a meal. You hollered and carried on, and your dogs were barking excitedly adding to the cacophony. Then you tried to make yourself twice your size by holding up your clothing above your head. Do you remember?' he asked smiling.

'That was you?'

Zeus laughed, but he said nothing.

'So, you missed out and were left feeling hungry?'

'No. I took a sheep from the next valley,' Zeus explained.

'Oh.'

'The next time I flew past, I saw that you had erected many stick men.'

'I called them, "Scare-men"' Ganymede advised him. 'They scare off predators as they get confused believing that they are adult men. We use them all the time now.'

'That was impressively ingenious of you,' praised Zeus.

Ganymede visibly swelled with pride. Any compliment from Zeus had to be significant.

'Over the years, I have watched you channel water from the river. You made it safer for the sheep to drink. You next brought water directly to your village. Instead of the hard toil of carrying the water, the water now flows into dams and it is for the benefit of everyone.'

Ganymede nodded.

'I live with many Gods and Goddesses in a place I named Mount Olympus.' Zeus explained.

'I have heard of it,' Ganymede confirmed. 'My parents think of it only as a legend.'

'That is how we prefer it,' Zeus informed him. 'Even still, we do tend to get a lot of human visitors. We are a mixture of immortals and humans. We mostly benefit from coexisting with each other and it generally works well.'

'But, why are you telling me this? Why are you here?'

'Good man. I am glad that you asked. Yes, we have a problem at Mount Olympus and your skill sets are perfect to remedy them. You must understand that our settlement has rapidly grown large. Water scarcity has become an issue. Our humans work tirelessly to bring sufficient water to us, but it just is not enough. Humans breed and their numbers are growing, but most of the Gods and Goddesses call Mount Olympus home. They do travel, and mostly they return to dwell in the luxury that Mount Olympus provides for them.'

'You want me to solve your water problem?'

'I would certainly be grateful if you did.'

'I do not know...' Ganymede hesitated.

Zeus pressed on. 'I will reward you by transforming you into a God. You will become an immortal, like me.'

Ganymede smiled trying to appreciate what that meant.

'You will retain your youth and live your life as an immortal,' Zeus explained.

'I am not sure… this…' he pointed outside, 'is my home… my family…' Ganymede blurted.

'By now your family believe you to be a sheep shagger,' Zeus countered.

Ganymede said nothing. He blinked several times as he considered the expression on Zeus's face.

'Why did you refuse the woman when she offered herself to you?' Zeus asked him.

Ganymede tried his best to explain. 'It would not be fair on her if I married her. I do love her, but only as a sister.'

'Is there another woman that you prefer?'

Ganymede hesitated thinking. 'No,' he concluded.

'So, you do prefer ewes, do you?' Zeus asked masking a smile.

'Definitely not!' Ganymede retorted angrily.

'Then do you prefer the company of men?' Zeus asked him.

'I have never been with a man. I have never been with anyone?' Ganymede explained.

'Does the thought of being sexual with a man excite you?' Zeus asked conversationally.

Ganymede blushed.

'Do you think of erect penises and feel aroused?' Zeus persisted.

Ganymede slowly nodded. 'I do,' Ganymede conceded and he then looked down at the floor. He was clearly embarrassed.

'Would you like to try it with a man?'

'What? With you?'

'Yes.'

'I couldn't.'

'Why not?'

'Well...' Ganymede hesitated. 'I have thought about sex with males, but putting it into an anus feels wrong. It seems... dirty.'

Zeus laughed. 'Men can be pleasured by other men without doing that,' Zeus explained. 'Few men enjoy having that part of their body penetrated. Besides, if done too often, it will weaken the anal muscles and that will lead to constant and embarrassingly unpleasant leakage.'

'So how...do they... you know?'

'When a man is with a woman and they have sex, it is called intercourse,' Zeus explained.

Ganymede nodded knowingly. 'His hard prick goes into her cleft between her legs.'

'Crude, but accurate,' Zeus confirmed.

Ganymede smiled.

'When men want to pleasure each other, they place their erect member here,' Zeus pointed, 'Between the thighs.'

'Oh,' Ganymede exclaimed now understanding.

'The main reason why it is so popular among us Greek males, is because human men are forbidden to engage in sex with a woman until they are married to her. I believe males pleasuring each other is also practiced in many other cultures. And they are doing it to bring both comfort and release. You see, it forms an indelible bond between the two men.'

Ganymede said nothing. He was learning so much from this God.

'Scholars call it intercrural sex, but it is mostly known as thigh sex,' Zeus continued. The rules between consenting males are complex and specific to their circumstances. The bond they form is often stronger than a bond between a husband and his wife.'

'Do married men do this too?'

Zeus laughed. 'Yes indeed, some married men also have this type of relationship. It is safer.'

'Safer?' Ganymede was confused.

'Women tend to become pregnant when having sex, or at least that is true for me, and far worse than that, women become jealous about their man performing enjoyable sex with another woman. In my experience, most wives do not seem to care too much about their man doing it with another man.'

'Why not?'

'I truly do not know,' Zeus replied looking somewhat bemused. 'I guess that for humans, male with male sexual relationships predate male female relationships. Also, men often find themselves away from female contact for lengthy periods. They go on hunting expeditions, or go to war, and they are away from wives for extended times. It is only natural for them to form healthy sexual associations with each other.'

Ganymede nodded his head agreeably.

'I guess also it is because you are not bothering your wife for sex all the time,' Zeus laughed. 'Men seem to want it a whole lot more often than the women do, believe me,' he laughed some more.

'I think I am beginning to understand,' Ganymede said hesitantly.

'Besides, solo pleasuring, despite being ultimately satisfying, is tiresome and lonely.'

'I agree,' replied Ganymede.

'That is good,' acknowledged Zeus. 'Now the thighs resemble the woman's parts when the other man holds his legs tightly together. It is the friction that stimulates you and you have an orgasm.'

'Orgasm?'

'When you spill your seed.'

'Oh!'

'Would you like to try?'

'Yes please!'

Zeus was quick to present himself to Ganymede and the young man performed the action on Zeus just as Zeus had described it. He ejaculated quickly, groaning with the pleasure of it. He then returned the pleasure by offering his clenched thighs to Zeus. Zeus also ejaculated quickly. They sat, exhausted, their seed spent. Ganymede laughed and Zeus laughed with him.

How do you feel?' Zeus asked cautiously.

'Great,' he answered. 'Relaxed and curiously lighter,' he added. He was smiling.

'That is good,' Zeus concluded.

'It is good!' It is great!' Ganymede was happy.

'It was good for me also,' Zeus confirmed.

Ganymede frowned and became serious. 'I hear that you have had sex with many women...' Ganymede began.

'I have,' confirmed Zeus. 'Being a God gives me much virility and I unquestionably enjoy a wide variety of lovers.'

'Do you have many men that you...?'

Zeus looked at him. 'Actually Ganymede, you are my first,' he informed him.

Ganymede smiled at the compliment.

'If you come to Mount Olympus with me, you will remain my one and only male consort,' Zeus assured him. 'Up until recently, my daughter Hebe has been my cup bearer, but she is now planning to marry Herakles, and she has become less devoted to my needs. You will become my cup bearer, do not worry, it is only ceremonial and we do not have many of them. You won't have to do much.'

Ganymede considered his offer. His choices were to remain here and be labelled a sheep shagger, or worse, be forced to marry Beth. Or, he could go to Mount Olympus with Zeus and be known as the shagger of the King of the Gods. He smiled at the irony of his choices.

'I will come with you,' Ganymede accepted with a gracious smile.

'You just did!' Zeus laughed at his own joke and Ganymede, confused at first, joined in.

'How do I get there?'

'With me, of course.'

'Are we walking to Mount Olympus? I thought you would want to fly there as an eagle.'

'I can alter my size as well as my shape,' Zeus informed him. 'You will climb on my back and I will carry you to your new home.'

Ganymede looked about him. 'What about my sheep?' he asked in concern.

'Yes of course,' Zeus agreed. 'They are your responsibility.'

Zeus went quite for a moment and then faintly spoke one name, 'Hermes,' he said softly.

Ganymede and Zeus stood examining each other for a moment when a younger, leaner, clean-shaven version of Zeus materialised in the shelter.

'Ganymede, this is my son Hermes,' he explained as he introduced the god to Ganymede.

'Hello, Ganymede. I too have been watching over you for a long time,' he informed him.

'You are the God of the flock.' Ganymede was clearly impressed to meet the God that his villagers had been praising and praying too all his life.

'Yes, I am.' Hermes confirmed. 'Among many other things,' Hermes added as he smiled.

'I forget who his mother is,' Zeus muttered.

'Maia sends her love,' Hermes smiled good naturedly.

'What do you call those nymphs that help you protect the flocks?' Zeus asked him.

'The Epimeliades,' answered Hermes.

'They help him guard the highland pastures and they are the true protectors of the flock,' Zeus explained.

'Among other things.'

'Nymphs often perform sexual favours for the gods,' explained Zeus. 'By the smile on Hermes face I would think him to be well satisfied.'

'There are no complaints from me,' confirmed Hermes, but he was not smiling as he walked outside.

Zeus and Ganymede followed him as some nymphs began to materialised onto the pasture. The dogs and the sheep were completely unaffected by their presence. The nymphs danced among them. Ganymede could see right through their clothing and see their nakedness underneath the thin fabric. They were beautiful and he could understand why many men would be attracted to them.

'Never challenge them to a dance contest, as you will lose,' Hermes advised.

Zeus turned to Ganymede. 'Ready?'

Ganymede looked about him one last time. He reached for his clothing and quickly got dressed. 'Yes,' he confirmed.

'It will be easier for you if I do this,' Zeus muttered. He bent down and got onto his knees behind Ganymede. He put his head between Ganymede's legs and positioned him up onto his shoulders. He then stood up and Ganymede wobbled uncertainly. Then the transformation started. Zeus started sprouting feathers and his giant arms morphed into wings, his head formed into the head of an eagle. His back became slippery and Ganymede had to hold onto the eagle's neck.

'Not too tight,' the eagle cautioned him.

'Oh, sorry,' Ganymede apologised and slightly relaxed his grip.

The eagle scrutinised the area, satisfied, it crouched and then leapt into the air, its wings flapping furiously as it lifted their combined weight into the sky.

As they ascended, Ganymede could for the first time, make out the full shape of the valley that he had called "home". He saw the village where he grew up. He could see people, but they were so small that he could not identify any of them. He accepted that they would now believe that he had run away, ashamed by what Beth believed she saw. The truth was that he flew away. There he was, on the back of a giant eagle that was Zeus, King of all the Gods, and that now he, a humble shepherd, was going to become a God himself! With a broad smile, Ganymede settled and enjoyed the journey.

Pan had promised him that his life would change dramatically. He could never in his wildest dreams or fantasies have predicted this out-come.

***

They arrived at Mount Olympus some hours later. Zeus flew several loops above the citadel so that Ganymede could appreciate the size and layout of his new home. Ganymede first observed the acropolis which was at the highest point of the settlement and it was the townships centrepiece. It was enormous and he had never seen such a bewildering structure before. It was surrounded on all four sides with massive rippled marble columns. Spanning the tops of the columns were massive triangular shaped beams that formed the roof. Every exposed surface was ornately decorated from scenes of the gods and goddesses performing their routine activities. It was magnificent.

Surrounding the acropolis are numerous oversized statues of the more senior gods and goddesses. Ganymede recognised them from the tiny replica statues sold in his home village market place. He was later to learn that this was often used as a meeting place of the high council and for other important civic functions.

The next remarkable structure that fascinated Ganymede was constructed with many steps that were shaped in a semi-circular pattern. At its base there was a flat elevated promenade and behind that was a tall wide structure with many windows and doors. He was later to learn that this was an open-air theatre, and it served to provide the Mount Olympians a venue for shared entertainment.

As they continued flying Ganymede thought that there must have been over two hundred formidable structures within the citadel's walled boundary, and within those walls there was still room to build more. He counted four gated entrances and each of these gates were wide open and they appeared to be unguarded. He could see columns of people that were either heading toward Mount Olympus or were leaving it. He also saw laden carts transporting everything from building materials, livestock, fruits and vegetables, bolts of fabric, and refined metals into the bustling home of the gods. Everything seemed orderly.

Outside of the walls of the citadel, there were thousands of simple homes constructed of rammed earth, timbers, and straw, and Ganymede concluded that this was where the humans lived. Apart from the main roads that led to each of the four gates, the paved passageways between the buildings were narrow and winding, and their haphazard arrangement sharply contrasted the carefully planned ornate street layout of the god's homes. He mentally noted the stark disparity in the living conditions between the gods and their worshippers.

Ganymede surmised that humans were only allowed to work or visit the inner workings of Mount Olympus, but that they were not allowed to live within its walled boundary.

They were now flying near to one of the gates to Mount Olympus. It was a tall wooden structure that appeared to be solid and stout. It also seemed like they had not been closed in a long time. Ganymede decided that the gods and goddess must feel secure and the threat of invasion or being overwhelmed did not feature in their thinking.

As Zeus was preparing to land, he spoke to Ganymede above the noise of the rush of air that had made normal conversation difficult.

'Do you see that large building with smoke billowing from the chimney?' Zeus asked.

'Yes,' Ganymede confirmed.

'That is the workshop home of my son, Heph. I will introduce you to him as I think you two will become friends,' Zeus concluded.

Ganymede said nothing, he was now concerned how Zeus's son will react to learning his father was having a sexual relationship with another man. He had already pondered the inevitable awkwardness of meeting Hera, Zeus's wife.

Zeus landed in a field that he had used numerous times before. There was no welcoming committee, no fuss. No one rushed out to greet them. The sight of Zeus as giant eagle, even when he was carrying a passenger, must have been performed often enough for it to be routine and of no interest.

As Zeus morphed back into his human shape, he gently lowered Ganymede to the ground. He pushed Ganymede off his head and they both stretched in relief. Ganymede noticed that Zeus was already clothed in his normal attire and he wondered what happened to them when he was in his eagle form.

They headed towards the buildings and streets that were to become his new home. There were large palatial homes that were solid one or two-story structures constructed from cut stone, bricks, and rammed earth. Ganymede observed that they were all in good repair, whitewashed, and they appeared clean and well maintained. Their roofs were uniformly made of terracotta roofing tiles, and they were in good condition.

The streets were paved with cut stones and were free of any litter or debris. Ganymede also noticed there was an absence of dogs and cats, or any other domestic animals which always featured within human settlements. The air was generally fresh, but he thought he could detect faint odours of humanity and he decided that they must emanate from outside the walls.

Ganymede spotted the drains immediately and he could tell that the engineers of Mount Olympus had thought of how to manage excessive water build-up on the streets during heavy rains and storms. The owners and residents of Mount Olympus obviously took great pride in their homes and their surrounds.

The streets were wide and there were trees and flowering plants in well tendered and ornately bordered gardens. The greenery of the plants contrasted beautifully with the whitewashed walls of the dwellings making everything seem vibrant in the radiance of the sunny afternoon.

Zeus cleared his throat. 'Hephaestus has some spare rooms at the back of his place,' Zeus informed him. 'You can live with him until we can find you a place of your own.'

'Oh,' Ganymede responded sullenly.

'Did you think you were going to live with me?'

Ganymede said nothing. He looked down and Zeus could see that he was despondent.

'Hera...' Zeus started to explain then dismissed the issue with a wave of his hand.

Ganymede nodded that he understood. He looked up and faced Zeus. 'How often will I see you?' he asked.

'When I can. You must understand that being the god of the gods keeps me exceptionally busy...' Zeus answered. He hoped that the young man was going to understand.

'You were saying about Hera?'

'What about her?' Zeus asked.

'How will she feel about us?'

Zeus suppressed a laugh. 'You will figure us out soon enough, Ganymede. Suffice to say my wife has suffered my many indiscretions, even since before we were married.' He studied Ganymede for a reaction, but there was none.

Ganymede had heard much about Zeus's numerous indiscretions as they were legendary. Common folk discussed them, and they exchanged gossip about them as readily as they traded goods. Humans thrived on stories of godly impropriety as they were entertaining, and their god's escapades took their minds off their own mundane lives.

It then occurred to Ganymede that he too would eventually become the subject of human gossip. Ganymede was now beginning to wonder about how much of his relationship with the king of gods would be spoken about by the people of these lands. He was not sure how he felt about everything that was happening as it was all unfolding so fast.

'Are you okay with that, Ganymede?' Zeus demanded.

'About you being with the other gods and your people?' Ganymede clarified.

'Yes.'

'You explained that the bond between males who practiced physical love was a sacred bond. It was to be taken seriously for the mutual benefit and trust of both of us.' Ganymede said squarely into Zeus's face.

Zeus smiled and nodded at his new young lover. 'I did say that,' he confirmed.

'I trust you, Zeus,' Ganymede told him.

'I promise you that you will be my only male consort, Ganymede,' Zeus assured him. After a pause he continued, 'As for other women... well, as a god I tend to pursue whoever takes my fancy, despite Hera's interference and disapproval.'

'Will she have any objection about me? I believe her wrath can be both intimidating and debilitating,' Ganymede said expressing his concern.

Zeus shrugged and offered an unconvincing smile.

'She won't like it, will she?'

'I would like you to stay at Mount Olympus until we find out,' Zeus suggested.

Ganymede cautiously nodded his acceptance of the arrangement.

Zeus opened his arms to Ganymede and they briefly hugged, much to the amusement of onlookers who had been watching from a respectful distance.

'Come with me,' gestured Zeus.

So, Ganymede walked the streets of Mount Olympus with his god lover. He felt he was now beginning to understand the dynamic of their relationship. He decided that he would be happy and satisfied with whatever time Zeus could spare him.

They walked past dwellings, shops, eateries, wine bars, and stables. There were fires burning and the smells of cooking. Ganymede now realised he was hungry. The assortment and quality of the foods on display for the shoppers to choose from greatly impressed him, though some of it he did not recognise. He was both intrigued and excited to be here.

Ganymede was delighted to be with Zeus as the numerous people they passed obviously loved and respected him. They greeted him with smiles, salutations, and sometimes even physical affections as they strolled by. If any were curious about Zeus's new young male companion, they were discreet enough not to ask.

Zeus next turned off the street and entered a building with a massive solid wooden door. He did so without knocking or even announcing himself. Ganymede looked about and then followed him in. The door slowly and quietly closed behind them unaided and Ganymede looked back and up to see that it was being gently pushed shut by a ribbon of uncoiling metal. They walked down a long passage, past sleeping rooms and kitchen adjoining a meals room and other leisure areas and into an expansive blacksmiths workshop.

They saw a middle-aged bearded man working on a metal contraption. He was so focused on his work that he had not seen or heard Zeus or Ganymede enter the room. He was busily reshaping the heated metal by striking it with a hammer.

Zeus waited for a break in the pounding before he spoke.

'Heph!' Zeus called to him.

The man looked up. He put down his hammer and the metal and came to them. He was wearing thick gloves, a long robe, and a heavy leather apron. His apron had scorch marks and was ripped in several places. He wore boots that had many scuff marks on them. He limped as he walked over to where Zeus and Ganymede were standing.

Heph and Ganymede both appraised each other briefly. Heph was politely curious about the handsome young man standing before him. He smelled of sheep and sex and he clearly needed to bathe. He was dressed like a sheepherder, but he must be important to Zeus if he brought him here.

Ganymede saw a sweaty bearded man who reeked from the hot iron-mongering work that he was doing. The smell of burning coals and molten metal was heavy in the air. Ganymede thought he saw a resemblance to Zeus in the man's facial features.

'This is Ganymede,' Zeus introduced them.

They nodded at each other, neither moving to shake hands.

'I would like Ganymede to make use of your spare rooms at the back of the house,' Zeus asked expectantly.

'As you wish,' Hephaestus agreed. He neither frowned or smiled at the prospect.

'You will need to gather some necessities for him,' Zeus continued.

Hephaestus re-examined Ganymede.

'What he is wearing, is all that he owns,' Zeus explained.

Hephaestus said nothing. He regarded what Ganymede was clothed in as old and disgusting.

'I will leave you two to get acquainted,' Zeus concluded. 'Look after him for me Heph, he is important to me.'

'Certainly,' Hephaestus agreed and nodded.

Zeus turned to Ganymede. 'Heph will see to you,' he explained. 'I have serious matters to attend to,' he continued. He then reached up and touched Ganymede's face in a show of affection for the younger man. 'I will visit you as soon as I can.'

He then turned without waiting for Ganymede to reply, and he strode purposefully out of the room, down the narrow passage and out the front door.

Ganymede examined the room. In the centre was a massive fire place. It had a bellows fashioned from timber and skins. Next to the fire there was also a large round water vessel. Adjacent to both was a large anvil. Hephaestus was working on this when they first came into the room. Near the anvil on a rack attached to a wall there were numerous blacksmith tools. There were also many other tools that Ganymede did not recognise.

Ganymede looked at Hephaestus expectantly.

'Come!' Hephaestus exclaimed abruptly. 'I will show you to your room,' he offered and walked off.

Ganymede followed him. They turned several corners within the building and eventually they came to a large dark green door. Hephaestus opened it and motioned for Ganymede to follow him.

Ganymede found himself in a large room. It was coloured a pale green and had murals depicting trees and plants. There was one window and the sun shone through brightening up the room. It had a large comfortable looking bed in the centre, and there was shelving for storing clothes and other such items. In an adjacent room was a bench with a bucket and soap and towel. There was another bucket on the floor with two lids on it.

'All the comforts,' Hephaestus said after Ganymede had surveyed the room.

'Thank you,' Ganymede replied gratefully. He looked about the room wide eyed. To him, a humble shepherd, this room was palatial.

'Zeus asked that I take care of you, so that is what I will do.'

'I appreciate that.'

'We are not particularly close,' Hephaestus explained. 'Unless he wants me for something.'

Ganymede already knew that fathers often behaved that way.

Hephaestus continued. 'You might already know this, but I was once married to Aphrodite.'

Ganymede studied the crippled man not sure what to say. He nodded imperceptibly. His doomed marriage to the sex goddess was legendary.

'I can see that you have heard of her.'

Ganymede simply nodded.

'My mother was against the idea, but I was besotted with her, so I married her against my mother's wishes,' he explained.

'Wasn't Zeus supportive?'

'Oh, he loved the idea. He helped me convince Hera and then arranged everything. He thought that by marrying a cripple, Aphrodite would be more controllable. He was wrong as she is truly an immoral goddess.'

'Oh.'

'So, father thinks me a failure for not being able to manage my wife.'

Ganymede nodded.

'Have you heard of Ares?'

'The God of war.'

'That's the one. He is my brother and he is also the main one screwing my wife.'

'So, she isn't here?' Ganymede asked.

'No,' he sighed heavily, 'She never is anymore. She may be known as the goddess of sex, love, and desire, but to me she is a slut and she should be described as the goddess of lust and infidelity.'

Ganymede said nothing.

'Ares and her have even sired some brats together,' Heph continued. 'Watch out for them. They are generally trouble for anyone that displeases them.'

Ganymede nodded that he would.

'Are you hungry?'

'I am,' Ganymede confirmed, suddenly realising that he was ready to eat.

'You will have to share my kitchen and fire,' Hephaestus explained. 'There aren't any cooking facilities in this room.'

They walked out of the room, back through the numerous passageways, through the workshop, through an extra wide double swinging door and into a food preparation area. Hephaestus poured a beverage from a pot into a clay bowl and handed it to Ganymede who accepted it, sniffing its contents.

'It's broth,' Hephaestus explained as he broke off a chunk of bread and handed it to the younger man.

Hephaestus motioned Ganymede to the chairs that surrounded a large wooden table and they sat near to each other. Ganymede ate hungrily. The broth was warming and tasted so good that he finished it quickly.

Without a word Hephaestus refilled Ganymede's bowl.

'Thank you.'

'So, tell me about yourself, Ganymede,' Hephaestus invited.

Ganymede told his host a condensed version of his life as a sheep-herder and how he escaped from being married to a woman he did not desire. He told him of Zeus's invitation to live at Mount Olympus and what Zeus had asked him to focus on when he had settled in.

Hephaestus was interested in the planned improvements to their public water supply. 'This is wonderful news,' he told Ganymede. 'There is much water in the nearby river, but I think we must extract it inefficiently.'

'I noticed you have taps in your kitchen. Where does that water come from?' Ganymede asked.

'Each home has its own rainwater storage urns. Zeus ensures sufficient rainfall so that our domestic supply never runs out. Our issues are with the water supply to public areas.'

'Can you construct public rainwater tanks?'

'Perhaps, but presently all the roofs are plumbed to capture water for internal use. There would not be enough for drinking fountains, water features, and bathing houses. Your improvements will benefit everyone.'

Ganymede beamed. He was happy that his mission pleased his new friend.

'And I will assist you,' Hephaestus told Ganymede. 'Tomorrow we will start working on improvements to the Mount Olympus water supply.'

'Hephaestus...' Ganymede began to ask. He seemed somewhat puzzled.

'Please, call me 'Heph,' Hephaestus invited.

'Heph, why doesn't your mother like Aphrodite?'

'Many reasons... I guess.' Heph speculated. 'Firstly, she is a Titan and generally the Gods do not trust Titan's since the war.'

Ganymede just stared at him. He knew little of the struggle between Gods and Titans.

'Besides, my mother dislikes competition and Aphrodite is an exceptionally desirable woman. Beware she does not try ensnare you into lustful submission. She would only do so for the control that she would have over you, and not for any romantic reason.'

Ganymede said nothing, but he thought that prospect highly unlikely.

'It is a long story and probably one that I will never truly understand, even though I am in some way one of its significant characters. I believe that my miserable attempt to become happily married to the most beautiful woman in modern times will be talked about for many years to come.' He smiled and paused in thought. 'The short answer is that she has become a lush. I am positive that she has bedded more men than Zeus has had women.'

Ganymede did not know what to say.

'In many ways, we Gods are no different to humans. When a male god, such as my father, has numerous conquests he is regarded as a stud, a legend, one who is respected by other males for his sexual prowess. But when a goddess behaves like a shameless immoral jezebel, as my wife does, she is regarded by the other gods and goddesses as a slut.'

'But we humans see her as the goddess of love and desire and sexuality.'

Heph smirked.

'Zeus and Aphrodite… have they ever…?'

'Those two!' Heph exclaimed shaking his head. 'Well, there's a thought. But I do not think so…. but I suppose if they ever were to do it, that it should not surprise me,' he conceded. 'No, I do not believe that it ever has, or ever will happen. She is not father's type.'

Ganymede and Heph continued their discussions for the rest of the day and into the night. Heph told him about the wars between the Titan's and the Gods and how, under Zeus's leadership the Gods had prevailed. They talked about Aphrodite and the effect his marriage breakdown had had on his happiness.

Ganymede described his upbringing as a shepherd boy and how he was destined for a marriage that he did not want. He then explained how Zeus rescued him from that fate. He left out the part of Pan's involvement and his trickery. He intimated that he and Zeus were more than just friends, but it seemed that Heph was neither interested or concerned, much to Ganymede's relief.

They later talked in great detail about the river and how to bring water from it into Mount Olympus with pipes and channels, creating fountains, bathing pools, wash houses, and taps for providing clean drinking water. Hephaestus was fascinated with Ganymede's ideas and he marvelled his understanding of moving water using only gravity, and that he had learnt this by himself, a simple shepherd boy.

Wearily, they finally agreed to "talk some more" in the morning. Before they bade each other a goodnight, Heph gave Ganymede several sets of clothes and a pair of sturdy shoes. 'My first gift to you. We can dispose of your old clothes tomorrow, and you can have a fresh start in your new home,' he explained smiling.

When Ganymede finally bathed and got into bed, his head was still buzzing from the stories of the gods and goddesses' battles and infidelities. And now, he was becoming a part of it. He hoped that when humans learned of his time here at Mount Olympus, that he was thought of kindly. He decided that he wanted to be remembered for his contribution to Mount Olympus's water supply, and not just as the only male lover on Zeus's list of consorts.

With Heph's help, he now believed he could do it.

***

The following morning, Ganymede awoke and dressed in the clean clothing that Heph had provided him. Heph suggested that they dispose of Ganymede's old clothing, as this was the opportunity for him to have a fresh start. Ganymede had quickly agreed that his sheepherder's attire was out of place among the gods.

He walked into the kitchen and found a door that led to the outside. He stepped through and found a waste receptacle and surrendered his old clothing and sandals into it. He suddenly realised that this symbolic act was all about acknowledging his new beginnings and not about lamenting his abandoned past life. He took in a deep breath and smiled.

He re-entered the kitchen and was startled to find a beautiful woman standing at the counter preparing some food. At first, he was worried that it might be Hera visiting her son, but he dismissed that thought as she seemed too young to be the mother of a god such as Heph. He then thought she might be Aphrodite, but he remembered their estrangement and also thought that it was unlikely to be her.

The woman looked up at him and calmly asked, 'Oh, who are you?'

'My name is Ganymede.'

The woman eyed him speculatively and she seemed pleased with what she saw. 'Are you a friend of Heph's?'

Ganymede did not know if he already qualified for that status, but took a chance anyway. 'Yes, I am using the room...' he turned to indicate the direction from where he had been sleeping, 'The green room ...just until I can find a place of my own.'

'That is a pleasant room,' she said as she smiled knowingly. 'And the bed is very comfortable.'

Ganymede nodded.

She held out her hand in greeting. 'I am Aglaia and I am one of the Graces and a Goddess of glory, splendour, and beauty.' she said and paused to judge his reaction. Getting none, she continued. 'I mostly help Aphrodite, but I also visit here to help care for Heph.'

'Are you and Heph...?' he asked leaving the question up in the air.

Aglaia immediately knew what he was alluding too and she smiled and shook her head. 'No, not Heph and I,' she explained and paused in thought. 'Heph is more like an older brother that I love and care for. He has two sisters, but they don't seem to visit him that often. Eileithyia does not appreciate him at all, and whilst Hebe adores him, she is too romantically distracted with Herakles at the moment, so they do not get together as often as they used too.'

'So, you work for Aphrodite.' It was more of a summation than a question. Ganymede said it just a way of learning more about her.

'I do, but I actually do not have to do much. We have enough human assistants who volunteer to do our cooking and cleaning. I am a bit of a party girl and I enjoy partying with Aphrodite,' she explained. She paused and examined Ganymede's face some more to gauge his reaction.

Ganymede suddenly felt he was being undressed with her eyes. Though flattered, he withheld a smile at the thought of her learning that he was not interested in women in that way.

'Do you like to party?' Aglaia asked coyly.

'I am sorry, but I do not know what a party is,' he answered politely.

She stared at him as if he was having a lend of her sensibilities. She next thought he was being playful and trying to lure her into making overt suggestions about being promiscuous together. She suddenly sensed an entrapment, that he was toying with her, and she felt excited about it. As she slowly reached up to touch his face her arm pressed against her clothing and she twisted her body slightly so that the action revealed more of her amble breast, almost showing her nipple. But as soon as she performed the manoeuvre, Aglaia was confused, as he did not respond to her reveal in the way all men do. She withdrew from him and stepped back. She then sighed and conceded that he genuinely did not know what it meant to party with a woman. Perhaps he was a virgin. She pondered the purity of an innocent male, and decided that it could be a lot of fun breaking in a new playmate.

Aglaia cleared her throat. 'To us goddesses...' she started to explain as she slowly stepped nearer to him, 'a party is when a girl and a boy like each other so much...' she was now face to face with Ganymede. He held is position as she continued. '... that they get naked and fool around.' She studied his face and then kissed him fully on the lips.

Ganymede let it happen, but he was no longer confused by what Aglaia meant by having a party with her. As she withdrew smiling contemplatively, his mind raced trying to think of the least offensive way to let her down.

'I am betrothed,' he explained calmly. 'Her name is Beth and I love her too much to party with another woman. Even one as stunningly beautiful as you are.'

Aglaia took several steps backwards. Her overtures for initiating sex with men had never failed her in the past. His explanation of promised fidelity toward another, while being lame in her opinion, also demanded to be respected.

She smiled and said, 'If you ever change your mind, I know that I could show a good-looking man like you a wonderful time.'

He did not doubt her.

Aglaia gathered the food she had prepared, picked up her beverage, and hastily left the room.

Ganymede felt pleased to have met Aglaia as she seemed affable. He was also impressed with himself by using Beth as an excuse not to be led into an awkward and undesired physical encounter. He silently apologised to Beth using her name in this way, but as she would never know of it, he believed he was in the clear.

Ganymede realised he was also hungry, so he set about finding some suitable food to eat. He found some olives preserved in olive oil. He ate a couple but it wasn't what he wanted for an early morning meal. He put the olive jar aside. He next discovered where Aglaia had put the bread. He broke off a bite sized chunk and dipped it into the olive oil and popped it into his mouth. As he chewed, he located two chicken eggs. He determined that they were raw by spinning them on the table surface and he decided he would fry them. There wasn't enough residual heat coming from the stove top that was used to cook food, so he opened the small door and inserted some cut timbers from the wood pile to reignite the cooking flames. He blew on it to get it started and soon the kitchen was filling with smoke. He shut the metal door and located the flange leaver to open the chimney. The smoke stopped issuing into the kitchen but some remained in the room. He opened the window and a gentle breeze greeted him and it quickly vented out the air in the kitchen.

He found a metal pan suitable for cooking the eggs and he poured some of the olive oil into the pan. He checked the temperature of the stove and decided that it was warm enough to start cooking. He cracked the eggs into the pan just when a beautiful woman entered the room. At first, he thought it was Aglaia, but she was taller and dressed in different coloured clothing, and she had different facial features. Though her hair was the same colour and styled in much the same way as Aglaia's, it was definitely not her.

She stopped and stared at him. 'Who are you?' she demanded.

He turned to face the questioner, 'I am called, Ganymede,' he replied, and turned back to inspect the progress of his eggs. He was concerned that he might over cook them as he desired his yellow yolk to remain runny, and he preferred the white part to be cooked firm. The timing was critical.

'What are you doing in Heph's kitchen?'

'Cooking these eggs for my breakfast,' he replied without looking away from the hot plate.

'I was not told that there would be additional people eating the food from this kitchen,' she declared. She seemed agitated

Ganymede suddenly felt guilty that he had opted to cook the two remaining eggs without finding out if he was allowed to do so. These eggs might have been the property of Heph, or someone else, and they may expect them to be available to them when desired. He turned to face the woman. 'I hope I am not interfering with anything that you were planning to do in here,' he said with a hint of trepidation.

'It is just that it is my job to make sure that Heph has enough food in the house,' the woman explained. 'I need to be told if there are any guests so that I can properly provide for them.'

'I see,' Ganymede nodded as he turned to face her. He too was often let down by inadequate communication, and he could sympathise. But he also did not want Heph to become the bad person in this equation, so he offered an explanation. 'My arrival yesterday was unanticipated by Heph, and also, it was quite late in the afternoon,' he explained.

Some of the tension left the woman's posture. 'I am Thalia, I help Heph with many of his domestic requirements.'

'I am pleased to make your acquaintance, Thalia,' he said sporting his best disarming grin. He knew from experience that by proffering his boyish charm, that it often tempered any ill feelings toward him.

'Your meal is burning,' she calmly alerted him to his problem.

Alarmed, Ganymede turned to see that his eggs were ruined. The yolk hardened and had turned gungy and unappealing. The egg white was blackened and scorched. Its future was disposal, and Ganymede now felt both guilty for wasting food, and bereft for missing out on something he had looked forward to eating. He removed the food from the heat source, opened the door to allow an even greater volume of fresh air to disperse the smoke. Disappointed, he performed a heavy sigh.

'Let me help you,' Thalia offered. She came toward him smiling benevolently and walking so gracefully that her feet barely seemed to touch the ground.

He smiled gratefully and stood aside with an exaggerated step and it caused her to laugh.

Thalia pulled aside the cabinet skirt to reveal a lidded waste receptacle. She pulled it out and Ganymede saw that it was seated on a gliding platform. She removed the lid and scraped the burnt eggs into the container. She replaced the lid, pushed the rubbish bin back into its position and adjusted the fabric. It was almost as if it had never happened.

She smiled at him and he returned her smile with a forced grin and a hapless boyish shrug.

'Would you like me to get some more eggs and prepare some breakfast for you?' she offered.

'I'm famished. Is there anything else I can eat?' he answered. He didn't want to appear ungrateful.

We can fire roast some bread and you can have it with honey,' she suggested sweetly.

Ganymede's face revealed his appreciation, and so Thalia set to work cutting bread and skewering slices onto toasting prongs. She held them carefully above the flames with practiced confidence and they slowly turned a golden brown.

'Will you be staying here long, Ganymede?' she asked charmingly. She felt some attraction for this young man, and now wanted to know more about him.

'I truly do not know,' Ganymede admitted. 'Zeus said he would help find me a place of my own, but he is busy and I don't know how long that will take. I don't want to be under Heph's feet for too long.'

Thalia laughed. 'Don't worry too much about Heph. He will appreciate the company. He hasn't completely recovered from the way Aphrodite treated him,' she explained sounding sad.

'Heph did mention some things about that. I guess I will hear more about her over time.'

Thalia nodded. 'So, you are here because of Zeus?' she asked, her eyebrows elevating to amplify her curiosity. The bread was ready and she placed it onto a plate and reached for a honey pot from a shelf and scraped honey onto the bread with a blade. She offered it to Ganymede, and he was both thankful for the food, and the opportunity to stall before answering. He took an appreciative bite from the honey bread and chewed contentedly.

By the time he had swallowed, he had formed his response. 'Zeus has commissioned me to improve the water supply. Heph is keen to assist me. We have already talked about doing it as a joint project,' he explained.

'Are you good with water?'

'It would seem so. I am also to become his cup bearer.'

'Hebe is too distracted with Herakles,' she nodded. 'Zeus must be fond of you.'

Ganymede swallowed nervously. 'Yes,' he conceded.

Thalia stepped up to him and stroked his face gently with her hand. With every word he spoke, she was becoming more attracted to him. Ganymede could sense what was happening and inwardly panicked. 'I have a fiancé named Beth.'

Thalia wasn't easily thrown. 'Where is she?'

'Back in my home village,' he replied.

'Will she be joining us here at Mount Olympus?'

'Err, no.'

'Will you be visiting her often?'

'Um, I think not at all.'

'Then she is no longer your betrothed,' Thalia concluded. 'By moving here, your bond with her is now severed.'

She reached up to pull his face toward hers as if intending to kiss his lips. Ganymede pulled away and spluttered. 'Actually, I am saving myself for my bride, please understand, it is not you, I'm just not into casual relationships.'

Thalia laughed. 'Ganymede, it was just going to be a welcoming kiss. I'm not going to force you into my bed and ravish you.'

Ganymede looked concerned. Her implication was that she wanted to someday bed him. 'I..., I..., look, I am pleased to know you. But I hope… that we can just… be… good friends.'

Thalia stepped back. She should have felt hurt from his rejection, but she wasn't. She quickly concluded that the poor boy was just incredibly shy. She suddenly loved him all the more for that. Most adult males spoil an emerging relationship by trying to rush her towards coitus. With Ganymede, she decided she could take her time, nurture him, and cultivate a genuine romance with him. 'Of course,' she said as if it were a welcome proposition.

Just then, another beautiful woman entered the kitchen. She stopped and stared at Ganymede. 'Oooh, who is this?'

'His name is Ganymede and he is a friend and a guest of Heph's,' Thalia explained. She turned to Ganymede and introduced the woman, 'This is Euphrosyne, she and Aglaia are the other two women who help me to look after Heph.'

Ganymede examined the woman. She was also tall and beautiful and had her jet-black hair styled the same way as the others. The colour of her hair was distinctive from the others, as was the hem of her dress which was short and billowy. It was easy to imagine that she wore nothing else underneath it, and for some unknown reason that thought was distasteful to him.

'If you like, I could take care of you also,' suggested Euphrosyne seductively as she walked nearer to Ganymede and looked ready to examine him. 'My, what strong arms you have,' she purred as she caressed them.

Ganymede felt he was a cornered rabbit shaking uncontrollably before a predator.

'You can try, Euphro, but he is saving himself for his wedding night,' Thalia advised.

'He is too young to be married,' Euphrosyne concluded and patted Ganymede smooth chin appreciatively. She preferred clean shaven men. 'Besides, he should learn some skills about pleasuring a woman before he commits himself to just one.'

'I will leave you to try your luck,' Thalia said without conceding that she already had, and failed. 'I'm off to get supplies for the kitchen. We are all eating here this evening.'

Ganymede wondered who that included, but he felt too timid to ask. He was suddenly uncomfortable with being abandoned by Thalia and being at the mercy of Euphro.

'I could come with you, Thalia. I could help you carry things,' he suggested.

'You are sweet to offer, but there are men at the market to do that. You stay here and get yourself better acquainted with Euphro.' With that, she headed for the door and left Ganymede to fend for himself.

Euphro smiled wickedly as she moved nearer toward him, but Ganymede thwarted her advance by asking her a deflective question. 'So, what are your roles in Heph's household?'

Euphrosyne paused her advance and took in a deep breath. 'I am an arbitrator. I help Aphrodite keep the peace between her and her numerous admirers. When I am here, I keep the disgruntled customers away from Heph, so he can concentrate on his many projects.'

'Does he get many complaints? He strikes me as a bit of a perfectionist.'

'Heph's work is excellent. He is a master craftsman. The problem arises when the client has unrealistic expectations. Heph is too nice to tell them that what they want is impractical or sometimes impossible, so he offers some promise that he will do his best, thus giving them an unreasonable expectation. When they are vocally disappointed, it is my job to pacify them when they come here all upset.'

Ganymede nodded and so Euphro continued. 'Thalia is our organiser. She manages the pantry and ensures that there is enough food and wine for the number of people expected. She knows how to organise musicians, entertainers, cooks, and waiters. She is especially good at anticipating the needs of others and so Aphrodite and Ares especially appreciate her for organising their numerous gatherings.'

Ganymede nodded.

'Aglaia is more of a party girl and so is great at cheering people up when things become dull. She is also gorgeous, but just remember that she is not as gorgeous as Aphrodite as she is the most beautiful and most desirable female that has ever lived. It is important that everyone know that you believe that to be true,' she cautioned.

'I will remember that,' he agreed.

'I do think that she and Heph sometimes spend the night together, but I believe that we are not supposed to know about it,' she explained and winked conspiratorially.

Ganymede nodded and Euphro took this as her cue to advance on Ganymede once more. He seemed startled by her advance and she paused. At first, she was confused, but then she was thoughtful, and soon she reached what seemed an obvious conclusion, all before Ganymede could speak. 'You prefer the company of males. You are not interested in the affections of a woman, are you?' she challenged.

Ganymede blushed, confirming her suspicion.

'Do the others know?'

He shook his head.

'Is it a secret?'

'I don't know.'

'Is it you and Heph?'

'No! Heph isn't like that,' Ganymede defended.

'No, he isn't,' Euphrosyne agreed and paused to think once more. Her eyes widened in realisation. 'It is Zeus. He has taken you as his lover,' she concluded open mouthed. Ganymede's blush confirmed her accusation. 'Wow, do the others know?'

Ganymede shook his head.

'Is it love?' she stared at him wide eyed in anticipation of his response.

Ganymede clearly struggled to explain his feelings for Zeus. 'I don't think so. It is just....' his explanation trailing off into nothing.

She had motioned for him to be quiet, and he gratefully stopped talking. 'Does Hera know?' she asked.

'I don't know...' Ganymede's voice petered out.

Euphrosyne thought he appeared miserable and distressed, and her heart saddened for the young man. He was a stranger in a strange land, in a unique relationship with the king of the gods, and he clearly struggled to express his feelings and desires.

She smiled benevolently toward him and rested her hands on his shoulders. 'I will explain it to the others, but rest confidently that none of us will speak of your relationship with Zeus to anyone outside of this household.'

Ganymede was relieved. His eyes had begun to tear up and the tears were threatening to flow, but her kindness, understanding, and assured confidentiality, relaxed him almost instantaneously. He took a deep breath and started to relax.

***

Later that morning, Ganymede and Hephaestus started their tour of the citadel of Mount Olympus. He was introduced to many human Olympians. Ganymede learned that humans were created by the gods to worship and serve. They generally work in the background as builders, cooks, cleaners, gardeners, and they faithfully provide for the Gods. They are for the most part, humble, grateful, and compliant. They live to serve them, and they enjoyed the aegis or protection of the Gods, mostly from Zeus and Athena. Therefore, they are rarely hurt, molested, or abused by any of the gods or goddesses. All the Gods and Goddesses know that Mount Olympus cannot function without humans, so respecting them and treating them right is the proper way to coexist.

The gods thrive on flattery and praise. It appeals to their vanity, boosts their self-esteem and it gives them their energy. As the human population grew, many people decided to leave the Mount Olympus region. Over time they set up many villages and towns. Soon, there were numerous thriving self-sustaining societies. The Gods are also more than aware that the numerous legends that have spread throughout the human domain, are the stories that former Olympian humans have shared.

The Gods passively encouraged human development, as it meant less work for them. With human expansion and innovation, there also came an increase in human expression. Art, poetry, song, and artifacts depicting the gods were crafted in increasing frequency and numbers. The humans were encouraged to thrive and prosper, as long as they remained subservient and completely devoted to their creators.

As they walked, Ganymede was introduced to many of the Gods and Goddesses that were presently residing or visiting Mount Olympus. Heph explained that many of them considered Mount Olympus to be their home, but they travelled and had adventures with other Gods and worked with the humans. Some especially enjoyed helping them, and only a few miscreants favoured hindering their progress. It was quite a mixed bag of interactions when you considered it.

But a few of the gods preferred to spend most of their time at Mount Olympus. Heph was one of them and another was his sister, Hebe who they were now meeting.

'Gany, this is Hebe, my sister,' Heph smiled as he introduced them to each other. Hebe offered her hand and Ganymede took it politely.

'Hello,' he said shyly.

'Hello Gany! I have heard a lot about you! The whole place is buzzing about you since your arrival,' she explained.

'Oh.'

'Do not be concerned,' she continued 'It's all good. Daddy has been telling everyone about how you will fix our water supply problems.'

'Oh,' said Ganymede, not sure if he should feel relieved.

'And with Heph's help I am sure you will have us swimming in fresh water quicker than I can fill daddy's cup.'

'Excuse me?' Ganymede asked, confused.

'Whenever there is a feast or a formal gathering, it is Hebe's job to make sure that Zeus always has a drink.' Both brother and sister laughed knowingly at an ongoing family joke.

Ganymede was confused.

'You see, Hebe only gives Zeus water in a wine cup. Other gods expect him to drink wine and to yield to its effects. Zeus loves wine and enjoys allowing himself to succumb to Dionysus influences. So, it is Hebe's job to pretend that she is serving wine, when she is actually keeping him sober.'

'Meanwhile everyone else is getting more and more intoxicated, confessing all their clandestine plans and practices to daddy, who is remembering it all for later when it really counts.'

'Wow!' Ganymede exclaimed impressed.

'Shush. It is our secret. It is now okay for you to know, you being so close to daddy and all that.'

'Oh,' he said. He was uncomfortable with how Zeus's family would react on learning the truth about his relationship with their father. But these two seemed okay with it.

'Hebe is in love with Herakles,' Heph added, changing the subject.

'Is he now living at Mount Olympus also?' Ganymede looked about him.

'He arrived just recently and he is still getting adjusted to being elevated into a God,' Hebe explained. 'Soon he will be all mine.'

'Oh. I would love to meet him.'

Hebe nodded enthusiastically indicating that it would be arranged.

'Hebe has been Herakles biggest fan. She plans to marry him,' Heph teased.

'Shush, Herakles does not know that yet,' Hebe cautioned, but she was smiling. She turned to Gany, 'I believe you will be taking my job as cup bearer.'

Ganymede nodded.

Heph decided to change the subject. 'Gany and I have been discussing building a series of water channels to flow into baths and drinking fountains,' Heph revealed some of their plans to his sister.

'That is fantastic you two!' she applauded happily. 'Can you improve on the fountain in the main arena? It will save us all a lot of bother.'

'Consider it done,' Ganymede promised her.

'And can you make a fountain that reminds us of daddy? I know he would appreciate that.'

'Sure,' Ganymede replied hesitantly, without actually knowing how to deliver on that promise. He looked at Hephaestus with a degree of uncertainty.

'We will figure something out,' Heph assured.

'Well, I must be off. Mother is expecting me.' She held out her hand to Ganymede who took it and shook it politely. Hebe laughed and pulled him into her, and she generously hugged him. She turned and walked off, leaving them standing there staring after her.

'Say "Hello" to mother for me!' Heph called after her, and she waved her acknowledgement.

Ganymede stared at him.

'Mother and I are still a bit estranged,' Heph explained.

***

They approached the only public fountain at Mount Olympus. They were near the central forecourt where significant gatherings took place to hear announcements and to witness significant events. The fountain was modest and only somewhat suitable for providing water refreshment. It had a crude basin which could be used to wash hands and face. The water flowed continuously and the overflow was mostly wasted as it splashed on the ground making it muddy. A stone gutter was supposed to channel it away so it didn't splash the feet of drinkers and it did capture some of the water.

'I think Prometheus was responsible for this fountain. I seem to recall that he had plans to provide for more, but that all stopped when father banished him.'

'I had heard that he had returned,' Gany queried.

'He did, but he now prefers to live on the outskirts of Mount Olympus, far beyond the walls, and close to his brother. We do not see much of him.'

Gany continued to examine the fountain. 'I think it has had better days,' he observed.

'There isn't much pressure,' observed Hephaestus staring at the drinking spout.

'And it is a shame that this water should be allowed to be wasted,' Ganymede added.

'See, it flows from here down past this wall and through this gap,' he pointed to the flow of water as it disappeared through a hole in the wall.

Ganymede jumped up on the wall to see where it flowed on the other side. He turned back to explain. 'It continues for a bit, and then it soaks away into the ground.'

'To have enough water to fill a public bathing pool, we will require a lot more water volume than this trickle.'

He jumped back down. 'Where does it flow from?' Ganymede wanted to know.

'I think it comes from the river,' offered Hephaestus. 'It is called the "Orlias," and it has plenty of water flowing in it all year round.

'Interesting name.'

'It means intuition and enlightenment. Oracles named it such because they believe in the powers of its waters. Apollo will know more about that. Before that it was briefly called the River Elikonas after the nearby mountain.'

'Have you ever seen it?'

'The mountain or the river?'

'The river.'

'I have, but it was quite some time ago,' he answered, now a little embarrassed at his previous lack of interest.

'Let's go and find it,' suggested Ganymede.

He jumped down and returned to the fountain and together they headed up the gentle gradient and followed the water channel carved from stone. It spilled over in many places making the pathway quite damp and slippery. They followed it as it meandered past many buildings and sometimes if flowed under pathways and bridges. The farther uphill they went, the greater the volume of water.

'A lot of water is wasted in this open channel,' observed Ganymede.

'It is,' agreed Hephaestus.

They came to the edge of the housing. The water course was cut into the rocky pathway and they followed it for quite a distance. As they came nearer to the river, they discovered dozens of women and men pouring buckets of water into the channel. They stopped and watched them toiling with a bucket brigade that was keeping the water for the God's fountain flowing. Now, other people were closing in on their position. Without a word the workers handed the buckets to their replacements who immediately set to work scooping river water and pouring it into the channel. Exhausted, those people who had finished their shift, now headed for their village.

Ganymede and Hephaestus intercepted them.

'Do you do this chore all day long?' Heph asked them collectively.

'Yes, my lord. But only during the daylight,' one of the women explained.

'We swap with the others when they come at sun peak.'

'For how long have you been doing this?' he asked.

'From when the builders first created the channel,' the woman explained.

'We have four teams,' explained another.

'We swap with each other throughout the day,' added the last.

Ganymede and Hephaestus stared at each other in disbelief.

On their return journey, they agreed they would find a way to automate the provision of water from the river to those who use it. Ganymede explained that he now wanted to learn all about how to build drinking fountains. He was interested in constructing pools of water for bathing, and he was now determined that none of the water was wasted. He would design a way to redirect this overflow water into agriculture, or to water the gardens.

By the time they met with Zeus they had detailed drawings and plans of what was needed to be done. Gany and Heph quickly received Zeus's authority to amass a significant human workforce to be tasked with the project. Numerous tradesmen were required to carve the stones that will support the channels that would be later filled with fresh flowing water.

When they had finished agreeing on the plans, Zeus turned to his son, 'Heph, could you please give me a moment alone with Ganymede?'

Heph nodded and left the room.

Zeus reached over, now gently holding Ganymede's face as he drew him closer and they kissed.

'I will be with you soon,' Zeus promised his young lover.

***

As the weeks passed, Ganymede and Hephaestus continue to map the citadel, adding more features to their drawings of how the water would best flow to reach vital parts of the city. Ganymede learned that the God's had sent some of the human Olympian's to Egypt to study architecture. It was there that they learned how to build Doric columns which were tall, elegant, and strong. They learned how to keep buildings in good repair, and how to pave streets so that the bricks stayed in place and that cambers were used to control the flow of rainwater and that they were properly drained. From what Ganymede saw, he felt confident they would find enough skilled craftsmen to complete the massive water supply improvements that they now planned for Mount Olympus.

Ganymede explained his intention for constructing a reservoir upstream from the current water source. He explained how they would cut a channel in the earth and divert some of the water from Orlias into the dam. There the sediment will settle and they would skim the cleanest water from the top and send it downhill towards the home of the gods.

Gany and Heph toiled over their drawings, sometimes late into the night. It was Thalia that ensured they got their meals, that they went to bed and slept, and she strongly reminded them that they still had a need to regularly wash themselves, despite their aqua preoccupation.

***

Most of the homes at Mount Olympus were adorned with stone carvings of the Gods and Goddesses. Sculptors carved free standing statues that were anatomically exact. They were obviously comfortable with nude male statues, but preferred that the female statues were carved wearing draped cloth. Ganymede found himself preferring it that way also.

Outside the citadel walls, the humans built modest homes for themselves. There were also several schools for military training and practice and these were often frequented by the God's themselves. There are also workshops for millers, bakers, weavers, garment assemblers, blacksmiths, potters, wagon fabricators, tanners, carpenters, stonemasons, and marble cutters.

There was also a plethora of artists and mosaic artisans who were employed to decorate the god's internal palatial walls with erotic art. It seemed to Ganymede that the residents of Mount Olympus were somewhat obsessed with expressions of lustful passions.

Many humans were engaged in food preparation, and the god's and goddesses ate well. Their gastronomic appetites always came first, but there was sufficient food production so that everyone was well fed. There were numerous tavernas serving a wide range of tuber vegetables such as turnips, carrots and radishes. They also grew cabbages, lettuce, garlic, fennel, and many other herbs. Baked goods were plentiful as were grapes. Everywhere you looked there were olives which were grown for eating and more importantly for its oil.

There are paddocks of lush grass for cattle, sheep, goats, and chickens. There were even fish ponds cut into the banks of the river and fish keepers ensured their feed, and regularly replenished their water using the nutrient enriched waste water for agriculture.

There were numerous vineyards that focused on wine production, and farms for growing food, and numerous large kitchens to cook them in. The Gods ensured the fertility of the soil and provided adequate rainfall so that the harvest was always bountiful.

The humans were encouraged to learn theatrics, music, poetry, dance, and song. They often performed for the Gods, much to their mutual delight.

Interestingly, there are no dogs, or cats at Mount Olympus. It seems that the Gods and their human workforce have no time or interest in them. When Ganymede discussed this with Hephaestus, he learned that there were no mice or rats either, but he couldn't explain why.

The human quarters were often visited by the Gods and Goddesses and they wandered freely among the people that worshiped them and served them. They often joined the human's audiences and watched human wrestling matches for amusement. They also presided over athletic and gymnastic events. The God, Apollo was a major patron of these events and awarded prizes to the winning Olympians.

Ganymede learned that there was little or no crime in Olympia. Potential offenders were quickly identified and were more rapidly expelled. A small group of soldiers routinely patrolled the outskirts of

Olympia and the God's themselves quickly intervened when trouble present itself.

But Ganymede was constantly dismayed by the amount of human activity required to transport water. The humans themselves washed downstream in the river, but the Gods preferred to have warm baths and the people had to heat numerous litres of water for each bathing pool. Water was boiled on site and tipped into the baths. When the water was too dirty, so they simply drained it and allowed to soak into the nearby soil. There, the weeds thrived and this was an additional chore for the humans to attend to.

Generally, it was a magnificent coexistence, but Ganymede believed that he and Heph, could improve it and make it even better.

***

Aphrodite and her son Eros were casually walking through the streets of Mount Olympus. They rounded the corner of a building and found that the path was blocked by a man and his mule. They watched as the man tried vainly to persuade the mule to stand and continue carrying its burden of food to the nearby eatery, thereby completing the man's assigned task. The owner of the eatery was offering suggestions that included striking the poor exhausted animal.

'Hit him,' shouted the eateries owner.

'He's just tired,' responded the man, horrified at the suggestion.

'Well, I must have that food in my kitchen! If you don't get this foolish animal moving soon, I won't pay you for your produce,' he threatened.

Aphrodite motioned for her son to assist.

'What! Why me?' he exclaimed at her, perplexed at her motives.

'Help them,' she demanded.

'Why?' he wanted to know.

'So that this man can have his produce and prepare meals,' she explained. 'So that this man can get paid and this animal can have a lengthy rest, which is what it obviously needs,' she told him, clearly impatient that she had to explain it at all.

'I will not,' Eros countered.

'Oh well, come this way then,' she motioned, turning to leave. 'We will walk the long way around.'

'No,' he protested and stood firm. Eros was upset that his mother had suggested that he, Eros, should assist moving a beast from their path. She had only proposed the detour because of him. Eros was not having it. He pulled his bow off his shoulder and knocked an arrow and drew back the cord aiming it at the animal's head.

'No!' pleaded the mule's owner.

'No!' chorused the eateries owner.

They positioned themselves between Eros and the mule.

'Move this animal, or I will kill it,' he threatened coldly.

'Eros!' Aphrodite scolded her son. 'Put that away!'

Apollo walked up to them all. Calmly and casually, he stepped up to Eros and pushed down on the arrow so that it pointed to the ground. Eros released the tension and both the mule's owner and the shop owner sighed in relief.

'Be careful, Eros. You might hurt yourself,' Apollo admonished him sarcastically.

Eros blushed in anger.

'Aphrodite,' Apollo said acknowledging the Goddess of love, beauty and sexual desire.

'Apollo,' responded Aphrodite smiling.

Apollo was the powerful god of music, art, poetry, healing, and learning, and she had yet to bed him. She admired the tall, muscular man. His hair was curly and always perfect as was his beard. He was the subject of many statues.

Apollo moved the animal's protectors aside and leaned into the mule's head. He whispered to it gently and caressed its neck and ears. It immediately it stood up and brayed. The mule next led its owner to the eatery, followed the eatery's owner and it then stood still patiently waiting to be unloaded.

Eros was not impressed but Aphrodite was.

'What did you say to that poor animal?' she asked him.

'I told him that if he didn't get up, that he would end up on the menu.'

Aphrodite and Apollo then both burst into laughter. Eros did not think it was funny.

'Apollo,' Eros spoke coolly when they had settled. 'I am having a few friends over this evening for a friendly game of Knucklebones. Would you care to join us?' he invited.

'Or you could keep his poor abandoned mother company,' suggested, Aphrodite smiling radiantly at him.

'Sorry,' Apollo apologised clearing his throat. 'This evening, I can do neither, as I will be dining with my father.'

'Maybe you will come by later. Or are you scared of losing?' teased Eros.

'I am not scared of you, or off losing. I just don't play games with cheats,' he told him coldly.

Eros tensed up.

'Eros does not cheat?' Aphrodite sounded perplexed at the accusation.

'Oh, he does. I pity the unwary and uninitiated. He often takes more than just their money.'

'Eros, why is Apollo saying these terrible things about you?' she demanded.

Eros was becoming angry and impatient. 'I happen to be good at games, mother. I like to wager and I generally win. I make no apologies for having fun whilst doing so. I never force people into the game.' He paused. 'Apollo is just a pitiful loser,' he concluded.

'Oh, I don't mind losing in a fair game,' he said as he let his words hang.

'Eros, please play fairly, even if it is not true that you cheat, you do not want to have a bad reputation.

'Mother,' he responded bowing his head in acquiesce.

'Don't believe him,' advised Apollo to Aphrodite.

'I will get you one day!' Eros threatened, reaching for his bow.

Apollo leaned in close to his face. 'No one likes a minion shyster,' he told him. Apollo turned and left Eros seething with anger, his mother's arm on his shoulder restraining him from enacting any type of retribution.

'Later my darling,' she told him.

***

Ganymede had briefly separated from Hephaestus to attend to urgent bodily functions. When he had finished, he traversed the narrow walk ways, and weaved in and out of the buildings in search of his new best friend. As he rounded a corner, he saw him standing near an eatery with a tall and very beautiful woman. As he approached, he noted that the woman was wearing a long lilac and translucent dress. He also noticed that she wore nothing underneath it, which seemed to be a common feature among resident goddesses, but not with the human females who dressed more conservatively. Ganymede had observed that Hephaestus had never discussed his desires for women with him. He also knew that he had no interest in males either, other than for friendship. Those males who preferred male intimacy were easy to identify, and they were never shy to express their desire to be intimate with him. Hephaestus had never done that to him, but then, he had not made any advances to the numerous women, both goddesses and mortals alike, that they had met during their time together.

Hephaestus saw him across the plaza and waved him over to join him. The woman looked up to see who Hephaestus was signalling too. As Ganymede moved toward them, she gave him a massively seductive smile.

'Ganymede, this is my ex-wife, Aphrodite,' he said dryly. Ganymede offered a hand in friendship, but Aphrodite brushed it away and pulled him in closer to her, his face somehow landed between her ample breasts in a hug that threatened to suffocate him.

Momentarily, he was able to break away from her and recover his composure. Aphrodite seemed disappointed. Generally, a hug such as the one she gave this handsome boy was enough to enslave them into unending love for her. This young man showed none of the normal "enamoured with her" symptoms that she so much enjoyed receiving.

Hephaestus smiled to himself. His wife could not resist a beautiful man like Ganymede, but Gany was able to resist her. He wanted to burst out and laugh into her cheating face, but he resisted the temptation. 'Ganymede is a consort to Zeus,' he said by way of explanation.

'Oh,' uttered Aphrodite in disappointment, her face contorted in mock pain.

There was an awkward silence between them all. 'Oh!' exclaimed Aphrodite once more in realisation of what that meant.

Hephaestus knew she was a quick-thinking seductress. He thought to himself that, that the second 'oh' meant that she had understood that her charms were not failing her, but that Ganymede was a man's man and therefore unobtainable.

'So....' she started, 'You... and Zeus.' It was more of a statement than a question.

'Yes,' replied Ganymede.

'How long have you been... err...together?' she tried to enquire politely.

'I have been in Mount Olympus for about two weeks now,' explained Ganymede.

'Two weeks!' she exclaimed. 'And already you are Zeus's consort.'

'Aphrodite!' interrupted Hephaestus. 'This is none of our business,' he scolded her.

She turned to Heph, 'You know my darling, you are absolutely correct,' she conceded. 'Where are my manners?'

Ganymede was unconcerned. 'I met Zeus at a place far from here. He invited me to come here with him, and we journeyed to Mount Olympus together. But he is busy and so I hardly ever get to see him.'

'Did you know that he is Hephaestus's father?' she revealed.

Ganymede looked at his friend.

Hephaestus said nothing but performed an imperceptible shrug.

'Zeus has many female consorts,' countered Ganymede. 'Are you one of them?'

Hephaestus nearly lost his composure.

'Zeus is a powerful God,' she replied by way of explanation. 'We do not do well together. In bed or out of it.' And with that she turned and walked away from the two of them.

Hephaestus led Ganymede around the corner of the nearest building. Out of sight from everyone else, he chuckled with laughter. Then it became a sustained laugh and he held his sides as if about to burst from the hilarity of it all.

Ganymede was somewhat perplexed. He started to laugh with along with his friend, without actually understanding why.

'I am sorry,' he offered. 'I have never been present to such a wonderful confrontation in all my married life.'

'I still do not understand why you were married to her,' said Ganymede.

'I became enamoured with her a long time ago. For me, it was love at first sight. She has always had a magical essence about her and I found her impossible to resist. I desperately wanted to have her as my wife.' He paused reflectively. 'And despite trying my best to please her, and doing my best to make it work, I did not succeed.' His head hung low.

'That is sad.'

'Aphrodite is a lying, cheating, manipulative bitch, and I was just the naive idiot who contrived and manipulated her into marry me.'

Ganymede said nothing.

'As you know, Hera is my mother.' he said to the younger man.

'Yes,' replied Ganymede.

'And you know that she is also Zeus's wife.'

Ganymede looked at him thoughtfully. 'I thought she was his sister?' He withheld a smile.

'She is that also!' retorted Hephaestus, 'We are an incestuous lot. That is why I have this limp,' he raised his lame leg as proof. 'It is a long story for another time.'

Ganymede nodded. He drew in a deep breath. ' And yet, Aphrodite, the most beautiful and desirous woman in the world, agreed to marry you.' he asked his friend rhetorically.

'Do you want to know why?'

'Yes.'

'To stay at Mount Olympus so she could torment my parents!' he explained. 'Both my mother and father despise her. He can have any woman he wants, but he will never have her, so he hates her,' He paused. Hera would happily banish her. So, to thwart them, she agreed to marry me, just to spite them in allowing her to remain living here.'

'Oh.'

'Oh indeed,' Hephaestus continued. 'As if that isn't enough, she is most often bedding my younger brother, Ares.'

'Oh.'

'Yes oh. And to make matters worse, I had to learn that fact from Apollo.'

'I have not yet met, Apollo,' Ganymede told him.

'He is my half-brother,' he explained, 'He is also one of Zeus's sons, but he has a different mother. He tends to be a kindly and benevolent God. He is super fit, exceptionally clever, and extremely handsome. I think you will like him.' He paused in thought. 'I do.'

'How is he with Aphrodite?' asked Ganymede.

'No interest. She mostly has desires only for Ares these days, and besides, Apollo already has his pick of women.'

Ganymede said nothing.

'She has two sons, you know.'

'Two sons.'

'Yes, there names are Eros and Anteros.'

'I have heard of Eros. Is he a winged god that inspires love with the gentle piercing on the intended with an arrow from his bow?'

'As legend would have it, but in truth he hides his wings well, and they are rarely seen. He has a potion that his arrows are dipped into, if he wants to inspire love between two people. He has other potions that can do harm.'

'And you are not his father?'

'No!' He paused. 'I am positive that it was Ares, but as expected, he denies it. Aphrodite won't say, and possibly cannot remember as she has been with so many males.' He paused and them grimaced. 'I just know it was not me.'

Ganymede said nothing.

'Because you actually have to have sex to make a baby,' he chortled on his explanation.' And on the few times I have experienced that with her, I know that it produced nothing of value.'

Ganymede smiled politely, but did not comment. He could tell that his friend was bitter and he felt sad for him.

'Come on,' suggested Hephaestus. 'Let us get some food. I'm starving.'

'Works for me,' agreed Ganymede. He was relieved that the topic had changed.

At the eatery they found that their regular table was available. They smiled as it was undeclared that it was their spot, and even when the place was crowded, it always seemed to be available for them to use. The serving staff knew from experience what to bring them, and they were quickly served and were now appreciatively eating.

'Hello Heph.'

Hephaestus glanced up and saw Eros looking down at them. He was on the second floor of the eatery and was calling down to him, waving.

'I am eating,' he said with a mouthful of food.

Eros walked down the curved staircase and sat in a vacant chair beside them. 'Who is this?' he asked examining Ganymede.

'My name is Ganymede,' he told him.

'Strange name.'

'I am rather fond of it.'

'How do you know this man?' he asked Hephaestus.

'He is both my friend and a close friend of Zeus,' Hephaestus cautioned him.

'Big deal,' Eros snorted.

Ganymede turned toward Hephaestus for an explanation.

'Eros.'

'Oh.'

'What do you mean by that?' demanded Eros.

'Your...' Ganymede paused unsure of how to title their relationship, 'uncle ... mentioned you.'

'He is not my uncle!' exclaimed Eros. 'And he is not my father either.'

'Yes, but who is?' Hephaestus asked casually and offered a smile. 'I would truly like to know.'

'Mother knows, ask her,' Eros said as a matter of fact. He then added after a pause. 'Besides, I do not want to know because as far as I am concerned, I am better off without him,'

Hephaestus believed that he did know, but he remained quiet. Eros had a nasty side to him, and as he was always armed with his bow and arrows, it was best not to trifle with him unnecessarily. Eros was known to be both playful and vengeful.

'Legend has it that the point of his arrows can exert a powerful influence on any person it penetrates,' Hephaestus explained to Ganymede.

Ganymede did not reply. They had just discussed this topic and he was curious as to where Heph was now taking the conversation.

Heph turned to Eros and asked. 'What do you dip your arrows in, Eros?'

'I have many potions,' he explained.

'But what is the one you use to drive people crazy with uninhibited passion?' Hephaestus persisted.

'I call it, Love.'

'Love!' harrumphed Hephaestus. 'You don't know what that is.'

Ganymede smirked.

Eros moved closer to Ganymede. Their noses were almost touching.

'When my arrow hits their skin, it leaves behind the uncontrollable desire for love,' he explained almost whispering.

'Is that right?' Ganymede whispered back. 'Doesn't it also wound them?'

'No. They remain unaware that it has happened.'

'Oh.'

'You see, I am just a humble match maker,' he added moving backwards. 'I assist the right people to fall in love with each other. I draw back my bow, and watch my arrow flow,' he motioned the action. He was smiling, clearly please with himself.

'You mean, fly?' Ganymede offered.

'Fly does not rhyme so well.'

Ganymede laughed but Hephaestus didn't join in.

'Do you play Knuckle-bones, Ganymede?' Eros asked.

'What are Knuckle bones?' he replied in a curious manner.

'Oh, it is a game we enjoy playing. I would be pleased to teach you,' he offered.

'Do not do it, Ganymede. He is excellent at it, and he will end up having all of your coin.'

'Oh, come on!' exclaimed Eros. 'This is untrue and unfair.' Then, after considering the situation he added. 'As Ganymede is a novice, I will teach him without any wagering.'

'Okay,' responded Ganymede. 'I am game. Where and when?'

'Tomorrow night. I will organise some others and we can have some fun. You can come too, Heph,' he invited.

'No thank you,' scorned Hephaestus.

'I cannot play tomorrow night. I have a mission to complete and it may take several days,' Ganymede explained.

Initially, Eros was suspicious that Ganymede might use this time to learn the game and ambush him with superior skills, but he dismissed the thought, remembering that Ganymede was a naïve novice at most things.

'Okay, let me know when you are ready and we will meet at a wine bar close to where I live,' he turned to Hephaestus. 'Heph will show you the way. He knows where I hang out.'

'I am looking forward to learning from you, but the water needs of Mount Olympus are my priority.'

Eros rose from his chair. He seemed satisfied that he had gotten his way once more. 'I will see you soon,' he promised as he was leaving.

'Ganymede!' Hephaestus exclaimed after Eros was out of ear shot. 'Why?'

'Remember that I was a shepherd before coming to Mount Olympus,' he said by way of an explanation. 'I have played knuckle bones all my life. I think we may have even invented the game.'

'Oh, is it time to raise some money?' Heph asked smiling.

Gany nodded and smiled confidently. 'And, perhaps I can teach Eros some humility.'

'That will never happen,' Heph countered as he stood up to leave. 'It must be time for us to go home and rest.'

'Heph,' Ganymede motioned his friend to wait. 'Tomorrow, I plan to leave here for a few days. I want to explore the upper reaches of the river.'

Heph nodded. 'That you can do on your own,' Heph said with a half-smile. 'My leg does not appreciate long walks,' he explained as they headed home.

***

The following morning, Ganymede set off up river. He had packed his carry bag with warm clothing as he had been told that it could get cool in the evenings. He also had enough food for a journey lasting several days. He had decided that he would explore the upper reaches of the river and if possible, find the rivers headwaters.

He soon passed through the diggings and saw the construction workers digging the ducts and dam that he and Heph had planned. The workers waved and greeted him cheerfully. They were now used to seeing Ganymede and respected his designs of the new ways to move water for the mutual benefit of the Gods and humans of Mount Olympus.

Despite being a warm day, the fresh mountain air kept Ganymede cool. A gentle breeze distracted the flies and so they generally clung to his back, and mercifully kept out of his face.

After many hours of walking, Ganymede entered territory which was new to him. He came across a long stretch of calm water. The river widened and he noticed that there were large fish in the river. He decided he would catch one and cook it up for his lunch. He unpacked the fishing net from his bag, stripped naked to save his clothes from getting wet, and slowly stepped gently into the water near where he had spotted his quarry. Standing waist deep in the water, he became motionless and focused, willing the fish to come close enough so that he could capture at least one.

There was a sudden movement in the vegetation behind him. He glanced around, but saw nothing. He was unconcerned that a wild animal might ambush him, so he returned his focus on catching a fish. Soon one came near enough and he cast the net, forcing it down on the unsuspecting creature. The movement caused Ganymede to lose his footing and he slipped bodily into the water. He came up spluttering but he had managed to trap the fish firmly in his net.

He then heard a chorus of female voices, followed by sounds of feminine giggling coming from the trees and bushes that bordered the river. Ganymede searched, but could not see anyone. He stepped out of the water, carrying the struggling fish in the net. The water streamed off his body catching the sun and making him glisten.

'Wow,' said a female voice.

'He is impressive,' agreed another.

'He is all mine,' declared a third.

'Where are you?' Ganymede demanded.

'Here I am,' announced the first voice as she stepped out of the bushes. She was a tall lean woman who appeared to be in her mid-twenties. She had long wavy auburn hair, a pretty youthful face, and unblemished tanned skin. She was dressed in a long free-flowing green dress that barely concealed her gorgeous body. She moved out into the opening and stood confidently in front of him.

'And I am here,' called the second. She was equally tall and beautiful. She had long straight blond hair that curled under her chin and her skin was slightly paler, but equally perfect. She was dressed in a thin, almost transparent blue dress of a similar design, and was also wearing nothing underneath it.

'Me too,' said a third woman's voice as she stepped into the clearing. She was wearing a brown dress in the same style as the other two. This one was equally tall, tanned, unblemished, and beautiful. Her lean figure showed clearly under her dress. She was a brunette with long curly hair that reached down the middle of her back. She stepped up closer to Ganymede and was smiling at him seductively.

'Who are you?' Ganymede asked in gentler tones, now accepting that there was no threat.

'I am Minthe,' said the first.

'And I am called Matope,' explained the second.

'And I am all yours,' offered the third while she positioned her arms on his shoulders, laughing at her own joke.

'That is a funny name,' replied Ganymede.

She laughed some more, 'No silly, my name is Daphne... but... I would like to belong to you,' she explained, wide eyed with expectation. The others approached him slowly and Minthe and Matope sat on the ground watching Daphne with Ganymede. She circled his body, gently sweeping her hand across his stomach and buttocks as she did so.

'Are you a God?' she asked him.

'No!' he answered quickly.

She circled him and placed her hand up to his chin. Turning his face gently she said, 'You look like a God.'

'Yes, yes,' the others chorused. 'He does; he does look like a God.'

'What is your name, handsome man?' asked Daphne.

'I am called Ganymede,' he offered by way of introduction. He moved away and reached into his bag and pulled out a sharp knife. Holding it firmly he slid the blade behind the fish's head, killing it. He then reached for his clothes in order to dress.

'Please don't,' begged Minthe.

'You are so beautiful,' claimed Matope.

'Please remain naked always,' Minthe pleaded.

'Er, no,' Ganymede said and slipped the top over his shoulders. He fixed his belt and stood clothed before them. He looked at them in turn as he said their names. 'Minthe, Matope, and Daphne. I have not heard of you. Do you live here, in these parts?' he looked about him as if to see a house or a dwelling of some sort.

'We do,' explained Minthe.

'We are Naiads,' added Matope.

Ganymede appeared confused.

'We are water Nymphs,' explained Daphne. 'We live here in the river all up to the way to the waterfall.' She turned and pointed and Ganymede looked in the direction, but saw nothing.

'Oh,' Ganymede said as he sat down on a fallen tree trunk and pondered the significance of this information.

'We guard and protect the river,' Daphne continued.

'Sorry for killing the fish.'

They laughed. 'Taking a fish for food is okay. We fish also,' Daphne explained.
'As long as our fish can breed and replenish, a small amount of fish catching is permissible,' Minthe explained.

'That is good,' replied Ganymede. 'I believe in that principle also,' he confirmed.

'Why are you here?' asked Daphne.

'To catch a fish,' answered Ganymede.

'There are plenty of fish downriver,' countered Matope. 'You don't have to venture this far from Mount Olympus to catch a fish.'

Ganymede laughed. 'That is true.' Then he added after a pause. 'I love watching the flow of water, and this river feels alive to me,' he explained. I want to learn all about it. I want to discover where the source of the river is for myself.'

'Why?' one of them asked.

'Like the fish that live in this part of the river, I want to be sure that the water supply is sustainable. There are more gods and people living at Mount Olympus than at any time in its history. We draw so much water from this river and I am concerned that it may not have the capacity to meet future demands.

Daphne walked behind him and knelt down. She hugged his back. 'Thank you for caring,' she told him. 'Most take this water for granted and we do our best to care for the river.' She moved over to the log and sat nearer to him. She ran her fingers through his hair. 'It is comforting to know that others care also.'

Ganymede rose from the log. He placed the fish into his bag and picked it up, placing the straps over his shoulder.

He faced the three of them. 'It was lovely to meet you all, but I must continue with my journey.'

'Aren't you going to eat your fish?' asked Minthe mockingly.

'Ahh…' Ganymede hesitated. 'Later,' he explained 'I am not hungry yet.'

He turned and started his journey upriver once more.

Leaving Minthe and Matope behind in the clearing, Daphne followed him. She turned and waved at them by way of explanation that she was going to spend time getting to know this handsome Ganymede. They laughed at her and waved back their support.

Daphne quickly caught up to Ganymede, and she grabbed and held onto his arm. 'Would you like me to guide you?' she offered smiling sweetly at him.

'No, but thank you for offering,' he replied.

Trying not to be put off, Daphne ventured, 'I could cook your fish for you.'

'It's okay. I can cook it when I am ready.'

She reached over caressing his stomach, moving her hand down his torso. Ganymede pushed her hand away.

She let go of his arm and stopped, but Ganymede just kept walking.

'Don't you like girls?' she wailed.

'I like all people,' Ganymede replied still walking away from her.

Daphne bemoaned her disappointment as she stood still, watching Ganymede recede from her. She threw herself around and stomped back to Minthe and Matope.

Ganymede smiled as he continued his journey inland. He liked the Naiads and hoped he would see them again on his return journey. He soon came to the waterfall that Daphne had described. It had cut a wide channel in the reddish-brown rocks and it poured down making an enormous noise as it bombarded the blue tranquil waters below it. He estimated the fall to be over twenty-seven meters high. He stood, mesmerised by its beauty. He initially decided that this would be a good place to camp for the night, but he changed his plan when he remembered that the Naiads also came to this place and he wanted peace and quiet. He camped further upriver after skirting the waterfall.

Ganymede walked for several days, catching fish for a meal when he was hungry. The forest thinned and the mountain air became cooler. He came upon a giant lake that was surrounded by snow covered mountains. It was quiet and it was cold despite the sun shining brightly on a cloudless day.

He drank from the water. It was chilly but pleasantly sweet, unspoilt by the rivers creatures that thrive in the water as it flowed toward the ocean. He knew it would be too cold to spend the night here, so he stayed for only a short while and then headed downriver toward home.

After two days travel, he came to the section of the river where he had first met the Naiads. He was a bit surprised not to see them when suddenly they burst up through the water's surface. Swimming toward him in the water they chorused, 'Hello, Ganymede, want to come for a swim?'

Smiling, he gestured his refusal.

They laughed and waved to him, motioning that he should join them.

Ganymede stopped walking and watched the three women ascend the river's edge and they were now standing before him, water dripping from their naked bodies. They stood provocatively, legs slightly parted, hips moving suggestively, as they casually asked him about his travels.

'Tell us where you have been,' demanded Minthe.

'What was it like?' asked Matope.

'Did you see anyone?' asked Daphne.

Ganymede was lost in their excited happy voices. He motioned them to settle and they sat down on the ground, cross legged, backs straight, and they were attentive.

He turned and sat on a nearby fallen log to begin his account. Not feeling the least bit uncomfortable being surrounded by three gorgeous and totally naked uninhibited women, Ganymede summarized the past four days of his journey. 'I saw the red-rock waterfall and I was truly mesmerised by it.'

They chorused an 'Aww.'

'I then followed the river for two days until I came to a crystal-clear lake that is surrounded by snow covered mountains,' he told them.

'Is it beautiful?' asked Minthe.

'It is the very wonderment of an almost frozen paradise,' he answered speaking softly as he was reminiscing. 'The air is brisk and Helios struggles to provide any warmth. The lake is fed by numerous streams and the water is so cold, yet when I drank from it, I found it to be sweet and pure.'

'I am also sweet and pure,' offered Daphne. 'You can sample me, if you would like too,' she offered enthusiastically.

Ganymede smiled at her. 'Thank you, Daphne,' he responded gently. 'But I must continue my journey home.'

'Why must you go?' Daphne pleaded.

'We could cook for you?' offered Matope.

'I have much to do in Mount Olympus,' he explained. 'And besides, Zeus is expecting me.'

The women went quiet. They knew that no-one, God or mortal, would choose to keep Zeus waiting. Ganymede stood and slung his bag over his shoulder.

'When you next come to Mount Olympus, you should come and visit me,' he invited, not certain of why he did.

'Oh, we never leave the river,' explained Minthe.

'We remain here to protect it,' declared Matope. 'It is our responsibility.'

'What type of trees are these?' he asked indicating the trees about him. 'They give off such a strong aroma.'

Minthe laughed. These are Laurel trees,' she explained. When you cook with the dried leaves they add much flavour to the food.'

Daphne went to a tree and selected mature leaves which she gathered in her hand. She walked to him and gently put them into his bag. 'Lay them out under the sun, and Helios will dry them out for you, and in just a few days they will be ready to use,' she explained.

'But do not eat the leaves,' cautioned Matope. 'They are quite bitter and a possible choking hazard, so it is best to discard them.'

'Thanks,' Ganymede said and he smiled his appreciation. He would pass them on to Thalia.

He headed off downriver toward Mount Olympus. He turned and waved and the three naked women waved back enthusiastically in reply.

'Goodbye, Ganymede,' they chorused.

***

Ganymede returned home and told Hephaestus about his journey. They concluded that the mountain snows will provide enough water to sustain the river despite their plans to draw from it.

Ganymede mentioned the Naiads in passing, but Heph wasn't that interested.

They set about designing many fabulous water features incorporating carved representations of the more significant gods in the design. The first one was of Zeus.

There was a knock on the door, and without waiting for an invitation, Eros admitted himself into Heph's workshop.

'Ganymede, I have set up a game for tonight, if you are available?'

'I am,' he replied looking at Heph.

Heph shrugged.

'Great,' Eros replied and he seemed pleased.

'I will show him where the wine bar is,' confirmed Hephaestus.

***

Ganymede and Hephaestus came to the front door of the eatery that was popular with serious Knuckle-bone players. The establishment served food, wine, and beer, and did well from the player's regular patronage.

'I'd better go in alone,' Ganymede explained to his friend.

'Seeing me with you will annoy him,' Heph confirmed. 'Best to keep the mood civil.'

'I will be okay,' he reassured him.

'I will wait for you,' Hephaestus offered.

'It will be a long night,' countered Ganymede, concerned for his friend.

'Are you sure you want to do this?'

'The silver I win tonight will help us complete the fountain.'

'We can always get more silver,' Hephaestus sounded impatient.

'That will take time and my way is quicker.'

Hephaestus studied his friend.

'And my way is more fun,' Ganymede added smiling.

'How many silver coins do you have?' He reached into his purse to offer Ganymede some additional coins.

'Just one,' replied Ganymede catching Heph's hand, preventing the gesture.

'One?'

'One is enough if I am winning, and too little to worry about if I lose.'

Hephaestus rested his hand on Ganymede's shoulder. 'Do well my friend, kick Eros' butt.'

Ganymede laughed and walked through the doorway and into the eatery.

Eros spotted him immediately.

'Ganymede!' Eros rose from the game he was watching to greet him. He was friendly, too friendly, and Ganymede felt it was best to be cautious.

'These are my friends.' He indicated to a group of middle aged, heavily bearded men, sitting in a circular pattern on the floor. 'That is Palus,' the man waved. That ugly one there is Eleni,' the man held up a cup of wine in salute. 'And the runt is Gasto.' The smaller man smiled and nodded. 'Dionysus couldn't make it this evening which is good, as you can take his place.' Eros smiled at him and slapped his back in a familiar fashion as he guided him to a place on the floor.

'So!' Eleni exclaimed. 'A newbie! A novice!'

Ganymede nodded in agreement, He felt he was grinning like a fool.

'A virgin player,' offered one of the others.

'Fresh pig fodder,' stated another.

They all laughed uproariously, and Ganymede just kept grinning enjoying the banter and the attention.

'These…' explained Eros holding up the five sheep's knuckle-bones in his hand, 'Are knuckle bones.' He passed them to Ganymede who accepted them and examined them with interest.

'The idea is to throw them into the air and land them on the back of your hand.'

Ganymede threw them up and caught two of the five in his palm. The others fell to the floor.

The men laughed at this. The smiled at each other knowingly.

'No,' Chided Eros patiently. 'On the back of your hand.' He gathered the knuckle bones and tossed the five into the air. He caught them on the back of his hand, and then threw them up once more and expertly caught them in his palm.

The others were impressed.

'Looks easy enough,' offered Ganymede.

The men laughed once more.

Someone called out to the barkeep. 'Bring some wine for our new friend.'

Ganymede collected all five knuckle-bones and threw them into the air. He managed to land one on the back of his hand, with the other four scattering noisily on the floor. He looked at the others, clearly disappointed with the result.

'You can do better,' someone encouraged.

Ganymede collected the bones once more and this time he landed two.

'Throw up those two and try and pick one up before catching the other two in your palm,' Eros bid him.

Ganymede did so and the men roared with approval.

'The newbie is learning, Eros!' They laughed once more.

Ganymede drank a large swig of wine just as someone slapped his back and he spilled wine from his lips and spluttered. The men laughed once more.

They played many games in this fashion over the next hour. Ganymede's skill slowly improved, much to the delight of the others, but he wasn't in their league, and it showed.

Progressively things quietened and then someone said 'I tire of teaching, lets gamble.'

'That would not be fair on Ganymede,' explained Eros patiently. 'He is our guest.'

'It is okay,' countered Ganymede. 'I will just watch you all play,' he offered.

'Are you sure?' inquired Eros politely.

Ganymede watched the betting for a while. He observed that they bet on the straight game and the silver being offered was small quantities. He laughed with them when someone had an unexpected win. Eros was slowly increasing the size of his pile at the expense of the others.

'Come on newbie!' challenged Eleni. 'Just one bet. You must have some coin on you!' he roared and the others bellowed their agreement and laughed loudly.

Ganymede felt compelled to wager. He hesitantly removed his one silver coin from his coin purse which he showed to his companions.

'One coin!' admonished Eleni.

'You will have to ask Zeus to increase your allowance,' teased Gasto.

Eros intervened. 'Leave him be,' he said calmly to his friends. To Ganymede he offered, 'I can lend you some coin, so that you can play.'

Ganymede paused before he replied. He seemed humble and uncertain of how to proceed. 'Thank you for your offer, Eros. I have one coin which I will offer in wager. If I lose, then that is just too bad for me. But I won't be indebted to anyone because of playing a game.'

'I respect that,' Eros replied smiling.

'Take his coin!' yelled Eleni.

Ganymede slowly placed the coin on the ground before them and looked at Eros.

Eros matched his bet.

Ganymede picked the first bone. Tossed it up and caught it on the back of his hand. Threw it up, scooped four and caught one. Tossed the five and caught them all on the back of his hand. Threw them up and caught them in his palm. He then calmly offered them to Eros. The men burst into drunken laughter.

'A perfect score!' Palus yelled.

Eros conceded the game smiling. 'Congratulations Ganymede, you have doubled your fortune.'

'Beginners luck,' Ganymede suggested.

'I agree,' said Eros. Re stake your pot and we will all match it, just to see you do it again.

'What? queried Eleni. 'Those odds are four to one,' he explained, but now he was not laughing.

'We have plenty of coin,' explained Eros. If he is any good, we will be helping him build his pot to something worth betting.

The others nodded their agreement and added coin. With ten pieces of silver in the pot, Ganymede repeated the round. The others watched in silence.

'I seem to have the hang of this,' he claimed as he offered the bones to Eros.

Eros conceded without comment.

'By Dionysus, I am thirsty!' bellowed Eleni.

Everyone laughed and the barkeep hastily refilled their cups of wine.

'You have played before,' stated Eros.

'No, it is just beginners' luck,' he countered.

'Teach him a new game,' suggested Palus.

'We call this one Aphrodite's hole,' explained Eros to Ganymede and he received an uproarious laughter from the others.

'I will demonstrate,' continued Eros.

Eros was right-handed so he formed a hole by joining his forefinger and his thumb on his left hand. He held it to the ground so that the top of the opening faced upwards. He threw one bone into the air, grabbed a second and put it into the hole and caught the first. He then repeated the action with the three other bones. He then handed the five bones to Ganymede.

'Challenge accepted?' he asked Ganymede eyebrows raised mockingly.

'Why do you call it Aphrodite's hole?' Gany asked.

'Because of the number of bones her hole has received,' Eros explained.

The men burst into laughter once more.

Defending Aphrodite against her own son's insult seemed ineffectual, so he received the bones without comment, as Eros added silver to the pile.

'Twenty,' announced Palus. 'That is a lot of coin.'

'Still feeling lucky, Ganymede?'

The others chuckled uncertainly.

Ganymede shaped the hole with his left hand and swiftly completed the challenge. He handed the five bones back to Eros who recoiled in unpleasant astonishment.

Someone forced out a curt laugh.

Eros drew in a deep breath. 'This one is called "Mothers hump",' he explained. He placed his left hand on its edge on the ground making a wall. He placed four bones on one side. He threw the other bone high with his left hand, and he then transferred one bone from one side of his left hand to the other, he quickly caught the falling first bone in his right hand.

'You have to do that with all four bones,' he explained to Ganymede as he handed them over.

Ganymede looked at him and then looked at the pile of coins. Eros also examined the pile and then counted out additional twenty coins and he doubled the pot.

Ganymede returned the bones to Eros. 'Thank you for the lesson, Eros. I have had much fun and it was a pleasure meeting you all. I have increased my fortune from one to twenty coins. I think my beginner's luck may come to an end on this one, and I could certainly use the silver. Ganymede stood up and gathered the pile of coins from the floor.

Someone laughed, but abruptly stopped when Eros glared at him.

He turned to Gany, 'So, my challenge is not accepted?' Eros stared menacingly at him.

'No,' he replied unperturbed.

'What if I made it more interesting?' Eros said reaching into his clothing and pulling out a money sack. 'I think there are about thirty coins in here.' He poured the coins from the bag offering to add them to the pile.

'Sixty,' said someone.

'Seventy,' someone corrected.

'I have never witnessed so much coin in one game,' someone else claimed.

'Challenge accepted?' Eros asked him coyly.

Ganymede sat down.

'I cannot match your raise,' he explained. 'And I will not borrow money.'

'That is why I am giving you generous odds, Ganymede,' he explained. 'Your twenty to my fifty,' he offered and then he indicated toward the others. 'These are your witnesses.'

Ganymede made the hump with his left hand. He placed four bones on one side. He tossed the first bone in the air and quickly moved one bone over his hand, and then skillfully caught the falling bone. He repeated this manoeuvre two more times, but on the last bone he fumbled and dropped the falling bone.

'Nearly,' offered Dimitrios.

'Well done,' encouraged Gasto, but his voice was soft.

'It is your turn, Eros,' Eleni stated.

Eros made the hump with his left hand. He placed the bones on one side of his hand and proceeded with the challenge. After the second bone was transferred, Eros threw up the third, but Ganymede witnessed that Eros had moved his left hand over the remaining bones to the completed side, all without lifting the bones over his hand. He had slid them to the palm side, but continued with the other actions as if he was doing it correctly.

'Eros,' Ganymede said calmly. You lifted your hand over the bones instead of the bones over your hand. You did it wrong.'

Eros blushed.

'I was watching your table hand,' Ganymede informed him suddenly aware of the tension in the room.

'Eros! Again, with the cheating!' Eleni admonished him. 'How could you? We have warned you about doing that.'

Eleni clipped Eros over the head. He had tried to duck but he was clearly embarrassed about being caught out.

'Barkeep!' yelled Eleni. 'Bring us a basket. Our friend has a fortune to carry home.' Turning to Ganymede he asked, 'Will you be safe with this lot? We can walk with you.'

Ganymede nodded. Satisfied, they helped him gather the coins and patted his back encouragingly. All the while, Eros sat staring glumly at his friends who were now assisting his new enemy. They gathered their possession's and moved out of the room, now ready to escort Ganymede home.

Ganymede alone remained in the room with Eros. He examined him in silent contemplation and then said. 'Thank you for teaching me the bones. This has been both an entertaining and rewarding evening.'

'You cheated!' claimed Eros dryly.

'I did not.'

'Not in the game. I think you deceived us by not telling us that you were already skilled with the bones. Beginners luck my arse.'

'A fool and his money are quickly parted,' responded Ganymede by way of a confirmation.

Eros said nothing.

'I was a shepherd before coming to Mount Olympus,' Ganymede added by way of confirmation.

'That speaks volumes,' Eros concluded.

'And besides,' he paused. 'I already knew that you would cheat,' explained, Ganymede.

Eros looked at him, now clearly puzzled.

'Apollo warned me that you had a habit of doing so. That is why when everyone was distracted with the bone in the air, I was watching your hand on the ground. By the way, if you hadn't of blushed when I accused you, they might not have believed me. You should get that under control if you decide that you want to continue to cheat other people.

Eros blushed an even brighter red, but he managed to remain composed as Ganymede left the room.

***

The following morning, as the sun was rising on Mount Olympus, Daphne had cautiously ventured into the citadel. She was hesitant and equally relieved that many people were still in their homes before the day's activities properly commenced. Daphne had only rarely ventured into Mount Olympus before now. She was scared of the hustle and bustle of the residents, proprietors, and tradespeople. She was also aware that her status as a water nymph did not offer her much protection should she be challenged by some of the more formidable gods and goddesses that inhabited the city. She was motivated to come here by her deep feelings for Ganymede. She was going to find him and she was certain that he would return the love and devotion that she felt for him, and they would become perfectly happy together.

She paused by a fountain and tried to get her bearings. It occurred to her that Mount Olympus was a big place, and that she did not know where Ganymede lived. She now decided that she would have to be brave and make enquiries without appearing to be desperate.

She was composing a reason to use when she asked about Ganymede's whereabouts, when a tall handsome god approached her. She recognized him as Apollo, spear in hand, as he came closer and smiled at her. Apollo was known to be the God of music, art, poetry, healing, and most of all knowledge, so therefore he should know the location where Ganymede resided.

'You seem lost. Can I help you?' he asked in a friendly manner.

'I am looking for Ganymede,' she replied shyly.

'Ganymede is a friend of mine,' he informed her.

Her heart leapt, but she said nothing, willing Apollo to continue.

'What do you want with my friend?' he asked her.

'We met, under pleasant circumstances, by the river several days ago…' she started, but he cut her off.

'And now you want to continue with your meeting? he asked sweetly.

'Yes, Apollo.'

'Oh, you know who I am,' he concluded seemingly pleased.

'I do. I am sure that everyone knows you. You do have an impressive reputation!' she told him.

'Well thank you. I hope it is deserved.'

She said nothing.

'What is your name?' he asked her.

Reluctantly she replied, 'Daphne.'

'Daphne,' he repeated. 'You are a water nymph, aren't you?'

'Yes. From the Orlias,' she turned pointing toward the river by way of an explanation. 'I live near the Red Rock waterfall.'

'You are beautiful, Daphne.'

Daphne blushed slightly but said nothing.

'I want to get to know you better,' he told her.

'By helping me look for Ganymede?' she asked hopefully.

Apollo sighed. 'Do you plan that he should fall in love with you?'

'I think so. Yes, I would like him too,' she answered.

'He is not actually interested in girls you know?' he asked rhetorically.

'I am a woman.'

'Yes,' he chuckled. 'I can see that.' He paused as he drew in a deep breath. 'I mean, he is not truly interested in females.'

'Does he not like them?' she was shocked.

'Oh, I am confident that he likes them,' he assured her, 'but not in the way that you are hoping for. You see, Ganymede is Zeus's consort. He is into male with male relationships.' His eyes widened and he hoped she now understood.

'Oh,' Daphne was clearly deflated by this revelation.

'I am sorry to be the bringer of disappointing news.'

Daphne said nothing. She fought back the tears swelling in her eyes. She did not want to cry. It was silly to come here and silly to think she'd find true love and she should return to her friends in the river.

'I am sure that there are others that you find attractive and appealing.'

She didn't understand that he was referring to himself. She shook her head.

Apollo seemed a little disappointed that she wasn't understanding his overtures but he continued. 'You look cold and hungry, and perhaps you might enjoy a meal and a warming beverage,' he suggested determinedly.

She looked at him blankly.

'Perhaps I could invite you, as my guest, to have some breakfast with me?'

She slowly shook her head.

Apollo looked disappointed. 'It is Ganymede or no one?'

She nodded expressionless in her agreement.

'It is a pity about Ganymede, but I do hope you change your mind about me.'

In the sudden realisation that Apollo was trying to seduce her, Daphne panicked. She blushed, mumbled, and hastily turned to leave. She was now feeling overwhelmed.

'Wait!' insisted Apollo, gently grabbing her arm. 'I didn't mean to worry you. You seem nice and I am attracted to you. I just wanted to get to know you better...'

'I have to go! I am sorry,' she said as she broke free and ran. She stopped and turned to examine him. 'I am truly sorry Apollo. Please forgive me, but I do not belong here.' She turned and fled.

Apollo felt crestfallen. He stooped and drank from Ganymede's drinking fountain and wondered what his young friend would think if he knew about Daphne's uninhibited desire for him.

As he sat by the fountains edge, he contemplated his next move. He didn't have much planned for the day. Pity, as it did appear promising for a brief moment. Daphne sure is beautiful. He hoped he would see her again soon, and that it would be a better outcome.

***

Eros was seated on the ground on the other side of the fountain. He had overheard the conversation between Apollo and Daphne without being observed. He now knew how to get revenge on Apollo for warning Ganymede about his cheating with the bones. Eros selected an arrow, dipped it into a pouch containing one of his special concoctions. This arrow had a modest point and was designed to deliver a negligible piercing of the intended's skin. It was also attached to a thin, light weight, but exceptionally strong line, so that the arrow could easily be retrieved. Once it hits its mark and delivers the drug, his arrow is discreetly withdrawn, leaving his victim none the wiser.

Eros knocked the arrow and drew the bow and let the arrow fly. It hit Apollo on his shoulder. He slapped his shoulder and scolded. 'Damn mosquitoes.'

Eros retrieved the arrow feeling quite satisfied with himself.

***

The potion that Apollo received had an immediate effect. It was now imperative that he find Daphne and seduce her.

***

Daphne ran through the city streets toward her river home. She soon tired and realised she was disorientated, hungry, and thirsty.

Feeling lonely and rejected, she sat on a chair next to a table provided by one of the eateries at Mount Olympus. Her status as a nymph granted her few privileges. They served her water and offered her a meagre meal in exchange for her one bronze coin.

She sipped from the water and was immediately aware that the water quality had improved since she was last here. Then she remembered that it was Ganymede who was responsible for that, and she burst into tears once more.

She could not understand his desire for a man, even if he was Zeus. She was resolved to give herself to him, and she had worked it out so beautifully in her head that he would happily reciprocate her love, once he got to know her better. But, as it transpired, she now accepted that it wasn't going to be. She sat, moist eyed, and alone in her misery and was unsure of what to do next. She thought that she might return to Minthe and Matope and resume her life as a guardian of the river.

She was about to leave when a man sat heavily in the chair opposite her. She sighed when she realised it was Apollo. Yes, he was tall and handsome and charming, but he was not Ganymede.

'Hello, Daphne,' Apollo spoke to her in his friendliest voice.

Daphne said nothing. She looked at him blankly, aware of her tear-stained face, but she decided to be unconcerned about her disheveled appearance. Maybe it will put him off.

'How can you be so beautiful and so terrible at the same time?' Apollo speculated gently. He was smiling reassuringly.

Daphne still did not speak. Maybe if she avoided talking to him, he would lose interest and move on to conquer some other more suitable woman.

'You are hungry, aren't you? Can I get you a meal?' he offered.

She shook her head. 'I have already ordered food,' she told him.

'I am hungry also,' Apollo declared. 'Do you mind if I get myself something to eat and join you?' he asked her.

'I was just about to take my food and leave,' she disclosed softly.

'Oh.' He paused considering. 'You ran away…'

'I was upset.'

'I promise you that I only have honourable intentions.'

Daphne didn't want to offend Apollo. He was a God of significant rank and power. She knew him to be kind and gentle, but she was not attracted to him. She wanted to be with Ganymede. She wished that this God would understand that and leave her alone. She stood up.

'I must go,' she pleaded in almost a whisper.

'Daphne,' Apollo spoke equally gently, 'Have I done something to offend you.'

Daphne thought that this was starting to feel pitiful, but she sat down again.

'Perhaps if you shared a meal with me, you could explain why you reject my most sincere advances toward you,' he invited once more.

'Please understand, I only have feelings for Ganymede,' she explained.

'But Ganymede is not that sort of man, Daphne,' he reminded her.

'No… I do not want to believe you,' Daphne replied with bitter disappointment, but clearly, she already did. She seemed crestfallen and rejected as she lowered her head in resignation.

'I don't…' she began and hesitated. 'I mean I haven't had many, much, I mean… I have lived a simple life by the river, and we don't see too many men and I don't actually have much experience with them,' she blurted and then abruptly stopped talking.

Apollo suppressed a smile. 'With Ganymede, the best you can be, is friends. For true love, romance, and passion, you will require a real man such as me,' he offered.

'I do like you, Apollo,' she told him. 'But not in "that" way.'

Apollo wasn't discouraged. 'I have much to offer,' he started his pitch. 'I am the God of music and poetry and I'm regarded as charming and sensationally passionate.'

'I do know your qualities, Apollo. You are a legend and are a great role model for the Greek people, and you are revered among the Gods themselves.'

'I truly do want you, Daphne,' his tone becoming more intimidating as the effects of the drug were now taking a greater hold of him.

'I can tell,' replied Daphne without smiling. 'You can have your choice of so many women, Apollo. Why do you want to seduce me? I have politely, and with the greatest of respect, rejected your advances. Why do you continue? You are the God of knowledge for Zeus's sake. With all your intelligence, why can't you figure this out?'

Apollo suppressed a smile. 'You have a good point, but my dear Daphne, the heart knows what the heart wants. Who am I to ignore true love when it presents itself so obviously to me?'

'I think it is some other part of your anatomy that wants me,' she told him.

Apollo reacted in mock offense.

'Have your meal, Apollo. With all that you have going for you, you will find a willing bed companion soon enough.'

She stood up once more ready to leave. Apollo reached up suddenly and pulled her down toward him. He thrust his face toward her in an attempt to kiss her, but she swung her head away and his face pushed into her hair. He stood and twisted her head toward him, but she dropped her weight and it caught him by surprise. She wriggled away from him and ran several paces.

Both Apollo and Daphne became aware of the crowd of onlookers that were now becoming interested in their activities. Daphne, panting breathlessly, performed a curtsy and turned to leave, intending to quickly get away from Apollo and Mount Olympus.

'Daphne, please!' Apollo begged. 'I love you!' he called after her.

She continued to walk speedily away, resisting the impulse to run.

Apollo stood and followed. Daphne was busy watching Apollo when she bumped into a man laden with bolts of cloth. She stumbled and fell to the ground. Apollo was there to help her up, but she was so frightened she again resisted. He dragged her up and bodily led her to an alcove away from the crowd. She became still and he tried a smile and held her in comfort and then tried to kiss her once more. She resisted forcibly, lifting a knee toward his groin. He deflected the attack but in the surprise of her resistance, he let her go. Stunned, he watched her flee, making no immediate attempt to follow her.

Apollo returned to the eatery and sat heavily in the chair. He was clearly suffering in anguish. He looked at the crowd angrily and motioned that they should quickly disperse and resume their previous activities. He took a deep breath and then sighed. She was correct. He could have any woman he wanted, including married ones. Being the son of Zeus had privileges and being a powerful god in his own right had many more. Why was he so besotted with Daphne? Why was he hurting the woman that he was professing to love. Why couldn't he ignore his feeling for her and move on? Questions..., so many unanswerable questions.

Apollo sat motionless as a thought formed in his mind. He would find Daphne and explain to her his true love and she would come to want him. He would make her understand. She had to. Resolved, he picked up his spear and moved off, fully intending on finding Daphne, and to always be with her, living a life of true happiness and unconditional love.

From a discreet distance, Eros had watched the proceeding with much amusement. He snickered and went off to find some friends to share his news with.

Apollo was not much for hunting, but he was skilled with a spear. It had many purposes, but mostly he used it to show off his skills and impress audiences. He had used it on the odd occasion to kill animals for food when travelling cross country, and he was never without it. He also knew that it served as a warning to potential protagonists. It was a natural part of him, an extension of his arm. He had often explained to an audience of delighted women that he'd "rather be naked than without his spear", and would arrange for all his clothes to fall to the ground as proof. On more occasions than he could remember, this "pick them up" technique had resulted in a satisfying intimate liaison.

Apollo travelled light. The river gave him water to drink and fish to eat. He left Mount Olympus in the late afternoon. He realised that Daphne had a solid head start on him, but he was faster and she did not know he would be following her so he was confident he would soon catch up with her.

***

Daphne ran like a woman that was frightened and in a hurry. The quicker she increased the distance between her and Mount Olympus, the safer she would feel, and the happier she would be. Daphne was both distressed and troubled by her encounter with Apollo. He had a reputation of being a gentle and kind god, and his behaviour toward her today contradicted that perception she had of him. She was torn between the news of Ganymede's alleged rejection of her, and of Apollo's display of unwanted and overt desire for her. She told herself to get away from him, and to stay well clear of the citadel. She would confirm Ganymede's interest in her, or the lack of it, in some other way.

Daphne followed the path around a bend in the densely treed area that was close to the river, when she came across Ganymede and Hephaestus and a team of labourers. They were working on a duct so that they could channel even more water toward Mount Olympus. Breathlessly, she ran up to him. 'Please, Ganymede,' she said pleading as she was trying to catch her breath.

Ganymede looked up in time to catch Daphne as she fell into his arms. He held her close to him whilst she shook and wept. Turning her face toward him he asked kindly, 'Daphne, what's wrong?'

'Apollo,' she blurted. 'He wants to…' she wailed and sobbed into his shoulder.

'Wants to…? Ganymede persisted.

Daphne started to compose herself. 'He wants to ravish me,' she exclaimed.

Ganymede said nothing. He looked at her. He believed that he knew Apollo well enough, and he believed that cajoling women was not his way of earning their affections. Gentle seduction was more his style, and he seemed to be the sort of male that was able to have his way with a woman whenever he desired her. He did not think that he would ever need to act forcibly toward one.

But clearly, Daphne, still shaking in fear, believed that to be true. She was genuinely scared of what Apollo would do to her. Despite not having any romantic interests in her for himself, he did like her, and he cared about her wellbeing. Due to her apparent confusion about Apollo, he immediately decided that he would help her and perhaps he might even learn the truth about Apollo's intentions.

'Apollo will be able to follow you, and he will find you easily enough,' explained Ganymede motioning her to see her foot steps in the soft soil.

'Will you help me?' asked Daphne.

'Yes, of course,' he assured her. He turned away from her. 'Climb onto my back,' he invited. She immediately jumped up onto his back, his hands catching her legs as she wrapped her arms about his neck.

Turning to Heph and the labourers he ordered, 'You… never saw her.'

'Saw who? asked Heph.

As Ganymede set off walking toward the river, Hephaestus and their labourers set about removing traces of their footprints.

Instead of continuing on the frequently used side of the river, Ganymede crossed through it on a shallower broader part, and he then continued downriver on the leafier and less used side. Daphne was about to protest when Ganymede explained. 'He will get confused when he loses your spoor.'

'Ganymede!' Daphne protested. 'Where are we going?'

'Apollo will be expecting you to run upriver and straight toward your home,' he explained. 'When he loses your tracks, he will get confused and become discouraged.' He stopped and motioned for her to get down, which she did.

'I will walk with you for a while,' he added. 'Until I feel that you are safe to go the rest of the way on your own.'

Daphne turned him with sullen and teary eyes. She now understood that Ganymede would only ever help her through friendship, but never out of love.

They walked together for some time when Ganymede stopped and turned to Daphne. 'I will swim across the river here and head back upriver. You continue downriver on this side for a bit longer. In a few days, he should have lost interest in you and you can cross the river and head home.

'Do you think I will be safe?' she asked him hopefully.

'Apollo has many female friends. I know him to be a kind and gentle god, and one that has great wisdom. I can't imagine him pursuing you to hurt you.'

'You don't believe me, do you!?' she spat out in disappointment.

'I believe, that you believe that you were in danger. That is enough for me to want to help you and to ensure that you feel safe,' he explained to her. 'I will send word to Minthe and Matope to come downriver to be with you.'

This seemed to satisfy her and she visibly calmed. 'When will I see you again?' she asked hopefully.

'When you are next in Mount Olympus,' he answered.

Dejected, she turned away and continued walking downriver. She heard the splashes that Ganymede made when he entered the water, and then she heard him swimming, but she forced herself not to turn around.

***

Initially, Apollo found that Daphne's footfalls were easy enough to follow. He was a skilled tracker but with Daphne it was like following a marked trail. She was heading closer to her beloved river and she was obviously making no attempt to hide her footsteps. The distances between her steps however were quite considerable, so he could tell that she was moving with great haste. He believed that she knew he was in pursuit of her, and he did not understand why she had rejected him and ran away, clearly frightened of him. He knew something was wrong, and he was determined to explain himself and set things right.

Apollo came to where Hephaestus and the labourers were working. Daphne's foot prints came to a sudden stop. He examined the ground for them, but there were none to see.

'I seek, Daphne!' he bellowed loudly.

Hephaestus looked up from the project. 'What is a Daphne?' he asked casually.

'Daphne is a she,' explained Apollo hurriedly. 'She is a river nymph and I am trying to find her.'

'Why?' asked Heph in a disinterested tone.

'I must apologise to her. You see, I was not myself when I made improper advances toward her.'

Both Hephaestus and Apollo were sons of Zeus. They didn't behave like brothers, and Zeus's offspring were so numerous that his children rarely behaved as siblings. But in this rare moment between half-brothers, Hephaestus saw in Apollo a genuine look of self-recrimination.

'Who were you?' he asked curiously.

'I.... I don't know.' Apollo replied. 'But I found this,' he indicated a small arrow wound on his shoulder blade.

'You think it was Eros?' he speculated.

'Probably,' offered Apollo. 'He would do something like this, just to spite me.'

'He is a trickster,' agreed Heph.

'Can you help me?'

'If I were seeking a river nymph, I would start by looking in the river,' replied Heph without committing.

Apollo examined him without expression.

Hephaestus pointed upriver.

Apollo gave him a brief wave of acknowledgment, and then set off at a slow gait. He followed the course of the water for several minutes but he could not reestablish her trail. He crossed the river, but could not find her footprints there either. He then remembered that she was at home in the water, so he concluded that she waded downstream, so he turned and ran downriver when he came across the trail of a shoed person carrying a heavy load. He was beginning to get an idea of what had happened, and so he raced downriver intent on finding her. The trail petered out again, so he re-crossed the river, when he suddenly came upon Ganymede striding purposefully upriver toward him.

'Ganymede!' said Apollo.

'Apollo,' responded Ganymede.

'I did not expect to see you,' Apollo stated in some confusion.

'Oh?'

'I have not observed any recent footprints,' explained Apollo looking at his feet, now understanding.

'I went downriver walking on the other river bank,' he explained and pointed.

'Oh.'

'You know me and water,' Ganymede smiled.

Apollo sighed. 'Have you by any chance seen Daphne?' he asked.

'Not for some time,' Ganymede answered truthfully. 'Why do you ask?'

'I want to apologise to her. I think I was under the influence of an evil spell from one of Eros's potions.' He then showed Ganymede the arrow wound that he had shown Heph earlier on.

'That would explain it,' agreed Ganymede.

'You have seen her?'

'Yes. You gave her quite a fright,' he told him after a lengthy pause.

'Do you know where she is now?

'No,' he replied as he shook his head.

'I will continue searching downriver until I find her,' explained Apollo.

'I think you should leave your spear with me. If Daphne sees you with it, she may think that you mean her harm.'

'I never travel without my spear!' defended Apollo. 'Everyone knows that! Besides, I would never hurt her.'

Apollo turned away and recommenced his slow gait downriver.

Ganymede turned and continued upriver. He was now fearful that Apollo might find Daphne and scare her once more.

After several hours of tracking Daphne, Apollo stopped and rested by the water's edge. He drank from the river, and then washed the sweat away from his face and arms. While sitting in quiet contemplation, he realised that he could hear female voices. He looked up and saw Daphne talking to two other equally tall and similarly gorgeous women.

'Daphne!' he exclaimed loudly.

Daphne turned and stared at him. After a momentary hesitation, she ran away, clearly frightened of him.

Apollo hastily rose and climbed up the sides of the waters edge to follow after her.

Both Minthe and Matope attempted to block his path, and Minthe even tried to trip him, but Apollo was too quick and agile, and so he jumped out of their way. He continued to give chase while calling out her name. 'Daphne! Daphne, please stop running! Let me explain!'

Daphne turned as she ran. She saw him, spear in hand, pursuing her. There was no way she was going to stop. She rounded a bend in the river when she came across her father, Ladon.

'Father, help me!' she screamed.

'What is it my child?' Ladon asked, alarmed by her tone and haste.

'Hide me!' she pleaded.

'Where?' he turned and searched about for a possible hiding place, but he could not see a suitable one.

Daphne was panting breathlessly and was also looking about them becoming exasperated. 'Change me into one of these trees,' she ordered.

Just then, Ladon saw Apollo far in the distance running quickly toward them. Ladon reacted quickly in an effort to save his daughter, and by lifting his hands in ascension, he commenced transforming Daphne into a tree.

She immediately became rooted to the ground. Her legs became numb and darkened, turning into bark. The bark reached up quickly consuming her body and quickly covered her torso and enveloped her breasts. Her arms and fingers stretched out and became branches. Finely, as her face and head were about to transform, she managed to whisper, 'please father, transform me back, but only when it is safe.'

Ladon, was surprised at the speed of the transformation. He heard a noise and saw the armed Apollo reaching his location. He turned and fled into the trees. But Ladon was old and slow, and so Apollo quickly caught up to him. Ladon stopped and while gasping for breath, he motioned his capitulation.

'Please, old man, where is Daphne?' asked Apollo.

'She is now one with the forest,' Ladon explained cryptically.

'What do you mean?' Apollo demanded. 'Where is she?'

'I have transformed her into a tree,' He explained proudly. 'Now, you cannot harm her.'

'But I never wanted to harm her!' he yelled. 'I am in love with her!' he explained.

'Chasing her with a spear in your hand is a strange way to show it,' admonished Ladon. 'She was running away in fear of you.'

'Who are you?' Apollo wanted to know.

'My name is Ladon, and I am Daphne's father.'

'Why would you turn her into a tree?' Apollo was bewildered.

'She ordered me too!' retorted Ladon. 'She wanted to hide from you!'

'Can you bring her back?' Apollo wanted to know. He was pleading.

'Yes,' he paused. 'At least, I think so.'

'Which one is she?' Apollo looked back at the hundreds of trees that densely lined the river.

Ladon slowly walked back to the water's edge with Apollo following. He stopped and commenced examining the trees in detail. He turned to face Apollo. 'They all seem to look so much alike,' he lamented.

'Can you find her?'

'I am trying,' he replied sounding desperate.

'What sort of trees are these anyway?' asked Apollo.

'Laurel trees. Some people call them bay leaf trees,' Ladon explained.

'Like that stuff that people cook with?'

'Yes, that is correct.'

'Have you found her?'

'I think so.'

'Why do you hesitate?' Apollo wanted to know.

'I must do this soon after she was first transformed, or the change will become permanent.'

'So do it!' Apollo demanded. 'Why do you hesitate?'

'But I only get three attempts at getting it right, and then my powers will cease to work, and it will be too late to save her,' explained Ladon.

Apollo motioned to speak but Ladon was holding up his arms toward a tree.

The tree's leaves instantly dried up and shrivelled. The branches quickly became brittle and several snapped and fell also. Next, they fell in a heap onto the ground. The tree suddenly fell over making a thunderous bang as it impacted onto the earth.

Ladon and Apollo jumped backward watching the remains of the tree dissolve before them.

'Oh dear,' bemoaned Ladon nervously. 'Wrong tree,' he explained.

Apollo said nothing.

Ladon approached another tree and affected the same result. Ladon turned pale, and Apollo became more worried.

'You must try again,' begged Apollo.

'But if I fail...' Ladon appeared miserable.

'You have no choice.'

Ladon approached a third tree. He turned to Apollo. 'This looks new,' he offered hopefully indicating the fresh bark and healthy green leaves.

Apollo nodded in agreement.

Ladon lifted his arms for a third time, but the leaves shrivelled and fell and soon after the tree fell heavily to the ground, its trunk quickly rotted away when it was no longer able to carry its own weight.

'Try again!' Apollo begged.

Ladon held his arms up to a fourth tree, but nothing happened.

Ladon sat heavily and Apollo sat beside him. The two men wept loudly for Daphne's sake, and for their own.

Minthe and Matope came up to them, and Apollo explained what had happened to Daphne. The two women joined the men with their tear-filled wails as they were also struck with grief.

After a while their sobs slowed, and they sat in silent contemplation.

Minthe began to look about the forest. She had an idea and she soon found Daphne's footprints leading up to a healthy Laural tree. 'This must be Daphne's tree,' she claimed. 'Look here at her footprints. They stop here.'

Both Ladon and Apollo were shocked at their oversight. The answer of which tree she was, was right there in front of them, and tragically, they missed it.

Apollo gathered stems of leaves from her tree. The three others watched him as he wove a wreath from the laurel leaves by slowly twining the stems and leaves into a circular shape.

Ladon looked at him questioningly.

Apollo cleared his throat. 'I am the patron of the Pythian Games,' he explained to them. 'From now on I will bestow all champions, a wreath constructed of laurel leaves in Daphne's honour.'

Ladon and the two women resumed their weeping as Apollo stoically set off to return to Mount Olympus.

***

Apollo returned to Mount Olympus burdened with a heavy heart. He found Ganymede and Hephaestus busily constructing yet another fountain. Their workers were completing the finishing touches, and water was now pouring in from the water duct. As the water fell from the fountain, it landed on a series of thin metal plates which produce loud, musical sounds. The rhythmic beat it produced was pleasant and comforting.

Ganymede explained to Apollo about their design. 'When Helios shines through it, the mist will light up with the colours of the rainbow. Iris has been helping us to get it right.'

'She would be pleased about that.'

'She is, we are also thinking of building a large fire lamp, so hopefully, the rainbow can be seen at night-time also. But it would only be lit for special occasions.'

Apollo nodded. 'I am impressed,' he told them.

'You don't sound impressed,' Hephaestus observed.

'You seem sad,' Ganymede added.

Apollo recounted the disastrous fate that had befallen Daphne and how he felt knowing that he was to blame. 'I just wish I understood what drove Eros to make me behave the way I did,' he sighed.

Ganymede held back his desire to remind Apollo that he had cautioned him about this possible outcome. It wouldn't help or change anything. 'Why don't we dedicate this fountain to Daphne?' he proposed. 'She loved water and...'

'I agree,' confirmed Hephaestus.

'That's a wonderful idea!' exclaimed Apollo. It won't bring her back, but it will ensure that she is never forgotten.'

As the three started making plans to honour Daphne's life, Eros, hidden from their view, had been listening to Apollo's story. He never intended for Daphne to perish, but he was glad that Apollo was miserable. He was pondering what to do next when he heard an urgent whisper coming from behind him.

Eros crept quietly to the whisperer, only to discover that it was Aphrodite. 'Mother?' he was confused.

'Shush,' she told him. 'I have just learned that Ares is on his way to fight in a fierce battle.'

'Oh. Why are we whispering?'

'I don't want Heph to know that we are leaving. Pack your things, we are departing soon.'

Eros was getting tired of her often-irrational thinking, but he capitulated gracefully and nodded. 'Yes mother,' agreed Eros. He resigned himself to her plan as the two were generally inseparable.

Ares, the God of war was Eros's father. But Ares was also Heph's brother and the main reason Heph an Aphrodite were estranged. To most of the other Gods, he was both feared and avoided. But he was enamoured with his mother and Aphrodite did not like to be separated from him for too long.

So, without any fuss or fanfare, Aphrodite and Eros discreetly departed Mount Olympus.

***

As the week's passed, life was fairly routine for the inhabitants of Mount Olympus. A young, athletic messenger from Zeus, ran hurriedly through the busy streets. He dodged a cart laden with stone, and then avoided a group of Goddesses whom were exiting a dining chamber having supped together. A street merchant offered to sell him an arrangement of flowers, but he waved him off as he ran past. The messenger knew the shortcuts, as there were many narrow passages constructed between the marble and stone palaces of the gods.

He found Ganymede at the construction site of yet another fountain. The area was partitioned from sight seers and the boy had to part the heavy curtains to find him. He looked up at the magnificent statue of their king, and he gasped in respect for the workmanship.

Hephaestus was at the other end of the statue, and he turned to see the panting intruder.

Ganymede paused from his work and examined the boy. He was mesmerized and Ganymede smiled. Their work was invoking the desired effect. 'Boy,' he called indicating that he should come nearer to Ganymede.

'Master, Ganymede,' the messenger responded having caught his breath. He approached Ganymede and bowed his head.

'You are not supposed to be here,' admonish Ganymede gently.

'I am sorry, but Zeus ordered me to find you.'

'Do you have a message for me?'

'Yes,' he answered without looking up.

'Well?'

'He invites you to attend to him in his bed chamber,' the boy spoke hurriedly and then bowed. He glanced up once more at the impressive statue of Zeus, and then turned and ran out through the curtain partitioning.

Hephaestus walked over to Ganymede. 'What did the messenger have to say?' he asked his friend.

'Zeus summons me,' he told him.

'Oh?'

'To his bed chamber.'

'Oh.'

'If he had asked me to meet him in the palace dining room, then I would know that he wanted to share a meal, talk, and generally catch up on things.'

Hephaestus said nothing.

'If we were to meet in the conference room, then it would be to discuss our work, and the progress we are making. He might even want to show some gratitude for all the water features, drinking fountains, bathing rooms, and janitorial systems that we have installed.'

'Mount Olympus certainly smells better,' observed Hephaestus.

'And the new public art is appreciated by everyone. I only hope that Zeus likes it also.'

'He is a busy God,' Hephaestus defending his father, passively.

'Yes, but it is to his bed chamber that I am required to attend, so there is no doubt about what he plans to do with me.' Ganymede was bemused but smiling. He was clearly happy about Zeus's plans for them.

'Our King of the God's has his needs,' Hephaestus added gently.

'As do I. I will be back as soon as I can,' explained Ganymede. I desire to have this completed today for the great unveiling tomorrow.'

'Take your time. There is not much left to do,' Hephaestus explained looking at their handy work.

Ganymede waved a curt goodbye to his friend and moved out through the curtained partition. He strolled casually through the streets of this wonderful place that he called home.

He reflected that Mount Olympus had the reputation of having more palaces, statues, and fountains, than any other place on earth. He lived here, and he helped make that true.

He eventually arrived at Zeus's private bedchamber door. It was locked, but Ganymede knew how to open the door. He pushed in on two separated stones and the door jamb was released. Ganymede pushed open the door and entered. He immediately pushed the door closed, resetting the mechanism.

There was a bathing vessel in the vestibule adjoining Zeus's sleeping room. It was already filled with hot water so Ganymede undressed and bathed. The rose scented water delighted him, and he smiled at his lover's passion for him. He was comforted knowing that he was Zeus's only male lover. To Zeus, women were a conquest, an adventure, a temporary plaything. Sometimes they were a challenge. But Ganymede believed that Zeus truly loved him, and that made him happy.

Ganymede dried himself with the soft towel. Still naked and pleasingly refreshed, he entered the bedroom and found Zeus, also naked, standing next to the bed.

'Ganymede,' Zeus purred.

'Zeus, my lord,' Ganymede walked over to him and performed an exaggerated bow. Smiling happily, he then entered Zeus's out stretched arms. Their mouths found each other, and they engaged in a passionate lover's kiss that quickly aroused both of them.

They sat on the bed, locked in a kiss, their hands reaching excitedly for each other.

Unknown to them, Hera was standing in the room watching her husband with his much younger lover. 'Zeus!' she called interrupting their pleasure.

They immediately detached and looked up at her. Ganymede stood up, his arousal clearly evident.

Hera studied him with curiosity.

'At least the modest parts of him know how to stand when I enter the room,' she smirked.

'What do you want, Hera?' Zeus spoke evenly. 'We are busy.'

'I can see that,' she chided.

'I love him...'

'Love?'

'You have never objected to him in the past.'

'Oh, I don't care that much about him. I accept that no individual person could ever satisfy your inexhaustible sexual appetites,' she concluded and smiled knowingly.

Zeus and Ganymede looked at each other but said nothing. Their mood had deteriorated.

'I came here to talk,' Hera said by way of explaining her intrusion.

'Now?'

'Yes.'

Zeus turned and stared forlornly at the younger man.

Ganymede smiled and gently kissed him, and then whispered into his ear, 'I will wait for you in the other room.' He then exited the room with a brief glance toward Hera. She ignored him as she was focused on her husband.

'Well. What do you want to talk about!' Zeus demanded. His tone indicated his irritation.

'I rather like Ganymede,' she said casually as she sat on one of the lounge chairs opposite the bed. She smiled. 'He is a handsome young man, and he has done a lot of good for the people of Mount Olympus.'

'You did not come here to talk about Ganymede's improvements to water features,' he said, his voice sounded gruff.

'No, I did not, you are correct.'

Zeus sighed. 'Get on with it.'

'Would you prefer to be dressed?' she queried.

'You have seen me naked before.'

'I have seen you naked many times before. You are a handsome man, Zeus, and I still enjoy seeing you naked,' she concluded.

'I am glad you think so,' he replied. After a pause, he added, 'And you are a desirable and beautiful woman.'

'Thank you. We have had a strong bond since you rescued me from father.'

Zeus nodded.

'Zeus, why did we get married?' she asked him.

'I think you married me to consolidate our divine power.'

'True, but why did you want to marry me?'

'For the great sex?' he ventured, his eyebrows raised as he smiled.

'I never had a problem having sex with my brother, and I agree that it is good. It is just a pity that we do not do it very often,' she stated.

'That is your choice,' he reminded her. 'I am always at the ready to make sure that you are well satisfied,' he assured her.

'I know I can get pleasure from you whenever I desire it,' she agreed. 'But I do not desire it very often because I know all about your infidelities and they sadden me, and diminish my passion for you.'

He nodded. He doubted that it was true, but it was easier to seem to agree.

'I have counted them,' she told him.

'How clever of you.' He was thinking she was talking about the number of times they have shared coitus.

'I may have missed a few...'

'You are very thorough.'

'But I am confident that I have it right.'

'A lack of confidence has never been a concern for you.'

'Did you know that you have fathered ninety-five children? And that forty-one of them are divine?' she explained, now examining him for his reaction.

Zeus remained quiet and said nothing. If he was surprised with the quantity of his offspring, he did not show it.

She continued. 'I believe that you do not celebrate their birthdays or even remember all their names.'

Zeus shrugged. 'I am not what you would describe as a "hands on" father,' he conceded.

'Not even with the four children that we produced together,' she reminded him.

'Well Hebe and I get along okay. Besides, I have been busy,' he countered.

'Yes, we were just talking about that.'

'How many of my progeny have you tormented?'

'Some,' she conceded. 'Mostly my vindictiveness was directed toward Herakles, but as you know, we have come to terms with each other.'

'How is he now?' he asked.

'He seems settled and happy with Hebe. His headaches are gone.'

Zeus nodded.

'Zeus, I am your wife.'

'So, what of it?'

'I should be able to come to you and talk with you whenever I want.'

'You do anyway,' he sighed again.

'I want you to stop fornicating with other women.'

'I have cut back,' he defended. But you already know that my proclivities are never going to completely stop. I have a habit of following my urges,' he explained knowing that it sounded lame.

'I know that,' she conceded and sighed. 'So, I want you to pleasure me.'

'That can be arranged.'

'Now.'

Zeus glanced toward the door where his young lover was waiting for him. 'I am sorry, but I am not really in the mood.'

'You were in the mood just now for Ganymede!' she snorted.

'I was, but...'

'So, pleasure me,' she demanded. 'I am your wife and I demand satisfaction!' She stood up and her clothes fell to the floor. She walked provocatively toward him, climbed onto the bed pushing him backward as she straddled him, her hips started moving in a gyrating motion stimulating him. Her eyes widened. 'See, it is already working,'

They were soon in full coitus. 'Oh, that feels so good,' she moaned as she climaxed, screaming loudly with the ecstasy of orgasm. She fell forward towards his chest, kissed him and then dismounted.

Lying on the bed, panting, sweating, she looked at Zeus and laughed. 'If you could see the expression on your face,' she laughed again.

Zeus rolled toward her and positioned himself on top of her. He entered easily and she immediately began to climax again. He focused on her pleasure and she orgasmed several times before he could not hold back any longer, and he spent his seed, arching himself in the intense pleasure of it all. Zeus was always silent when he came. He collapsed, resting his weight on Hera. They were both breathing heavily and she pushed him off of her.

Hera smiled at her husband and then turned onto her side and moved her leg over Zeus's. Her hand clasped his limp member. She teased it and worked it deftly with her fingers.

He stared at her. 'What are you doing?'

'Again,' she demanded softly as she smiled looking seductively at him.

'Really?'

'Yes!' she insisted as she giggled.

He took in a deep breath. 'Give me a moment,' he said as he smiled. Soon his member was responding. It was good to be a God.

As soon as Hera decided he was firm enough, she mounted him once more. He was deep inside of her and she was soon moving in an urgent frenzy. The waves of orgasmic pleasure began surging through her body. Finally, she collapsed in a heap next to him. She laughed and squealed in feminine delight.

She rolled unto her stomach, lifted her body off the bed into a kneeling on the all-fours position. 'Enter me from behind,' she instructed.

He moved into position behind her.

'Properly,' she reminded him. 'Not like how you do it with Ganymede.'

'I know what I am doing,' he assured her.

He pushed into her once more. She moaned with delight as she quickly climaxed. His thrusts intensified and finally he ejaculated once more. His energy was spent and he dropped exhausted onto the bed next to her.

She laughed at him. 'Is that all you have got?'

He appeared puzzled. 'That is all there is. I am spent.' He took a deep breath and then laughed at her.

'No,' she looked deep into his eyes smiling. 'Please sir, can I have some more?'

'I cannot,' he told her.

'I bet you would for Ganymede.'

'Is that what all this is about?' he asked incredulously.

'No,' she answered and smiled, but she knew she didn't sound convincing.

'It is! You are jealous of him.'

'I am not.'

'You are.'

'When will you tell him that he is a Trojan prince?' she asked deflecting his words.

'Never.'

'Why won't you tell him?'

'I worry that he may run off on some damn foolish quest to reclaim his birth right.' He paused. 'He would probably get himself killed for nothing.'

Hera said nothing.

'Besides,' Zeus continued 'He is happy here.'

'I promise that I will say nothing,' Hera assured him soothingly. 'But only if you are a gentleman and indulge your wife once more.' She studied him with wide-eyed anticipation.

'Again?' Zeus looked pained. He studied his wife seemingly confused. 'But we have already had plenty,' he explained.

'Yes, and now I want more of you,' she told him.

He drew in a deep breath. 'Can we wait until tomorrow?' he asked, his eyes pleading.

'No, I want you to pleasure me now,' she explained motioning toward his flaccid member. 'Get him up for me please,' she instructed.

'I don't think I can,' he stammered.

'Are you a god or a wuss?' she teased.

'I am empty!' he explained.

'I want more!' she demanded again and started fondling him.

'Look, if you can make it grow again, you can have more,' he offered, smiling. 'Otherwise, you will have to wait until I have regained my strength.'

He somehow managed to oblige her, and when she decided he was stiff enough, she mounted him once more. Her pleasure came quickly and she fell into a heap on top of him. It was in this way that they both fell asleep.

Sometime later she stirred and woke him by kissing him passionately on the lips. She lifted her head and gazed into his eyes and she softly demanded, 'More,' she whispered.

They rested for a while. Over the course of what remained of the evening, she managed to mount him several more times. Her climaxes were decreasingly modest, but she seemed as pleased as the cat that had found and licked the cream. Zeus however, could not climax again, as his seed was truly spent.

When finally, Hera stood up and looked at him she smirked, 'Not a bad effort for an old boy,' she told him. She kissed him once more, then gathered her robes and exited his bedroom.

Zeus lay on his back exhausted. He was puzzled by Hera's behaviour. This level of sexual appetite for him was truly out of character. He speculated that she wanted to prove something to him because of Ganymede. Ganymede! He had almost forgotten about him. Zeus rose from the bed and winced in some discomfort. He walked to the chamber where Ganymede was waiting. He entered the room and found him sound asleep on a pile of pillows and blankets. He watched Ganymede and smiled. He was so beautiful and he regretted not being with him this evening. Zeus turned and returned to his own bedroom. He washed meticulously and then lay down on his bed. He soon fell into a deep exhausted sleep.

***

When Zeus awoke, he found Ganymede in bed next to him. He smiled and caressed the younger man's face. Ganymede woke and smiled lovingly in response.

'I am sorry about last night,' Zeus apologised.

'Hera is your wife,' Ganymede spoke softly. 'A husband should respond to his wife's desire for affections.'

'I am glad that you understand,' Zeus spoke softly.

'I have a surprise for you,' Ganymede said as he sat up in bed.

'No.' Zeus implored, 'Not that. I can't.'

Ganymede laughed. 'No, it's not that. Your surprise is outside,' Ganymede explained to him.

'That's good,' Zeus replied relieved. 'What I need now is food and fresh air.'

They dressed and moved into the dining chamber. Servants had prepared food for them and they ate hungrily. They finished and walked out of Zeus's palace and out into the street. They walked in relative silence, Ganymede leading the way.

'There are many sleepy heads this morning,' Zeus observed.

'What do you mean?' asked Ganymede.

'The streets are quiet. There is no-one about,' he explained as he gestured about him. 'They must still be in bed,' Zeus concluded.

'Or...' Ganymede smiled, 'They could all be here, waiting for you to see your surprise!'

They rounded a corner and Zeus found himself among a large gathering of Gods and Goddesses and some favoured mortals. They cheered him, and he raised his arms in salute of their praises.

As the crowd parted, Zeus could now see a giant cloth covered centre piece in the public square. Ganymede waved to Hephaestus who ordered workers to remove the covering cloth. A giant fountain statue of Zeus was revealed. The water appeared to fly from his fist in a burst of pressure. It caught the sunlight and flashed brilliantly. The water struck a mounted plate and the thunderous sound it made delighted the crowd. They cheered and applauded as each burst of water, caught the light as a show of lightening, and then splashed on the metal making the sound of thunder.

Zeus was impressed. He embraced Ganymede in appreciation.

A celebration brunch had been arranged, and the revellers moved toward the tables of food and drink. The party lasted all day and was still going strong as the evening approached. Even Hera joined them and she seemed happy and delighted with her husband, his fountain statue and even of Ganymede.

As darkness enveloped the festivities, many of the merry-makers were now dozing in slumber. Zeus commanded everyone who was still awake to listen to him. 'Be quiet, give me hush!' he bellowed.

They respectfully quietened and were now attentive to hear Zeus's announcement.

'Ganymede, you have done me proud.' His speech was somewhat slurred with the wine. He indicated to the newest fountain to feature at Mount Olympus. 'The contribution you have made to the people of Mount Olympus is truly wonderful. You have provided us with numerous drinking and bathing fountains and have generally done a lot of things.'

'I had help,' Ganymede indicated Hephaestus.

'Heph is a truly gifted man, son, God, whatever,' Zeus was exceedingly drunk. He smiled benevolently and waved to Hephaestus.

Heph smiled and returned the gesture.

'As promised, I am making you immortal, Ganymede. You are now a God! You are the "water bearer!" he bellowed 'Look' Zeus pointed to the heavens.

Everyone looked up. Ganymede wept with joy as he realised that his Zeus had commanded the heavens to arrange the stars into a new constellation of "The water bearer", which is now know to us as Aquarius.

'I thought he would appreciate it,' Zeus explained to the gathered crowd who laughed.

Ganymede thought he heard his name being called out, and so he looked over his shoulder to see Hebe and Herakles waving at him, and he smiled and waved back.

He was tapped on the shoulder and he turned to see Heph, Thalia, Aglaia, and Euphrosyne, all queuing up to offer him congratulatory hugs. He was happy to receive them.

Later, when he and Zeus were alone, spent from their intimacy, he further surprised Ganymede with the news that he had named of one of his planet's moons after him.

Zeus explained to him in a loving way, that he wanted them to remain close together for all eternity.

***

Novella one - the constellation Pisces

The ancient Greeks identified and named Forty-Eight out of the Eighty-Eight recognised constellations. They were catalogued by a Greek astronomer Claudius Ptolemy in his publication the Almagest around 150 CE. The origins of the mythological stories that identified the constellations predate this documentation by as much as a thousand years.

Novella one - the constellation Pisces and the story of Aphrodite and Eros, the Two Fishes.

Aphrodite is well known as the Greek goddess of love, romance, and sexuality. Aphrodite is also known to us as Venus, and the planet is named after her in her honour. This is the story of how Aphrodite came to be. Born in the ocean during a struggle between father and son, she was raised on an island. As an adult she was carried by Zeus to Mount Olympus to work and play with the gods and goddesses who resided there.

After a brief marriage to Hephaestus, she formed a steamy relationship with Hephaestus's brother, Ares and they had a son they named Eros. All her life, she struggled with the unwanted, yet amorous advances of the Titan monster named, Typhon. Eventually, she and Eros had to flee Mount Olympus to escape his wrath, and they eventually became the constellation of the Two Fishes, known to us as Pisces.

This book is now available

Novella two – the constellation of Capricorn

Novella two – the constellation of Capricorn and the story of Pricus the Sea-Goat.

Pricus is an old sea-goat with a problem. He is regarded as the old man of the sea. The younger generation wants desperately to abandon the old ways and leave their ocean home to live a more adventurous life on the land. The sea-goats are able to morph from sea-goats into land goats when they emerge from the surf to walk on land. They quickly learn to morph into human form, and to their delight discover that they can have much more fun exploring the plethora of opportunities that await them. In their naivety they make many mistakes, some ending in tragedy. Pricus is desperate to save the younger generation from themselves, and so must become increasingly resourceful do so, and do so in a way that his solution remains permanent. His dedication to his own kind earns him his place as the constellation of the sea-goat, known to us as Capricornus or Capricorn.

Planned launch 2026

Novella three - Saturn's moon Pandora

Novella three - Saturn's moon Pandora and the story of the first human woman.

Zeus, king of the Greek God's, commissioned his son Hephaestus to craft the first human woman. Aided by Athena, he carefully researched the perfect form and then moulded her from clay He then painted and glazed her into the perfect woman. After being fired in his kiln, she was given the breath of life by the wind god Zephyr. She was named Pandora, being the bearer of the gifts bequeathed to her by the gods and goddesses of Mount Olympus. Her main purpose for humanity was to become the role model for all future human women. Zeus then commanded that she be properly trained so that she can navigate life's complexities, but her tutors do too good a job with her, and she becomes too powerful for a normal human life. Zeus became disillusioned with her and he decided that she should be married off to a minor god, so that she'll do no harm to herself, or to others.

Pandora's story is so significant that she is honoured as Pandora, one of Saturn's moons.

This book is now available

Novella four - the constellation Taurus

Novella four - the constellation Taurus and the story of the Jupiter's moon Europa and her meeting with the white bull.

When Zeus, king and master of the gods and goddesses of Mount Olympus finds himself between wives he sets out on a desperate search for the perfect woman to marry. On a sunny field, set among spring flowers, on a stretch of land adjacent to the sea, he finds her. She is Europa, a gorgeous African princess. For Zeus, it becomes love at first sight. In his infatuation for this woman, he tries numerous times to impress her, and almost succeeds. Sadly, for Zeus, his one true love is betrothed to another, and sadly for Zeus, a daughter must do her duty. Disguised as a magnificent white bull, he tries one last desperate attempt to have her. The consequences of his quest for true love are celebrated as the constellation of the white bull, know to us as the Taurus.

Also commemorated in this story is the constellation Draco, known as Ladon the Dragon. Also featured is Laelaps as the constellation Canis Major or Greater Dog, and the Teumessian Fox as the constellation Canis Minor or Lesser Dog.

This book is now available

Novella five- the constellations Scorpio & Orion

Novella five- the constellations Scorpio & Orion and the story of the scorpion verses the hunter.

Artemis is the goddess of the forests and of the hunt. She befriends a hunter named Orion. Their friendship is slowly progressing toward a blossoming romance when Orion boasts of his ability to wantonly kill all the animals that cross his path. Artemis is dismayed. Her policy is to only kill for food, to kill for pleasure is an outrage. She feels she must sacrifice her future relationship by stopping Orion from completing his boast. She manifests a giant scorpion and sends it to attack and destroy Orion. A massive battle ensues and both are defeated, thus   preserving animal life from indiscriminate killings. To celebrate the outcome and to remind us that all life is precious, their images are cast into the heavens as the constellation *Orion* and the constellation of the Scorpion known to us as *Scorpio*.

Planned launch 2025

Novella six - the constellation Aries

Novella six - the constellation Aries and the story of Chrysomallos the Ram.

Born from a union between Poseidon and Theophane on a remote island that was the home of a flock of sheep. They are interrupted by shepherds during copulation, so they disguised themselves as sheep to avoid the embarrassment that Theophane might suffer if their tryst became public knowledge. Their male child is born with the ability to morph from human form into a ram. From his father, he has long golden hair, and when he becomes a ram, he has golden fleece. He has wings and the ability to fly.

He is named Chrysomallos and he is raised by his loving mother Theophane. He eventually befriends princess Helle who live in a nearby kingdom. When their lives become perilous, Chrysomallos the flying, golden fleeced Ram, comes to their rescue. His bravery is celebrated as the constellation of the Ram, know to us as *Aries*.

This book is now available.

Novella seven - the constellation of Ophiuchus

Novella seven - the constellation of Ophiuchus and the story of Asclepius the serpentius or serpent bearer.

Asclepius was the son of Apollo. When Apollo had to rescue Asclepius from his dying mother's womb, he realised that he did not know enough about medicine and surgery, and so he set about discovering as much as he could. He later taught all that he learned to his son. Next, to further his education, Apollo decided that Asclepius would learn even more from the tutor Chiron. Through him he completed his training and went on to be the foremost authority on how to manage illness and repair injuries. His wife Epione and he had five daughters and three sons, and all became involved in the practice of medical treatments. The most prominent daughter was Hygieia and the practice of hygiene is named after her.

Both Apollo and Asclepius have been forever revered as the fathers of medical treatments and their names were included in the original Hippocratic Oath, that all medical practitioners swore upon when becoming formally registered to become doctors.

His dedication to healing the sick and injured was commemorated in the night sky as the constellation *Ophiuchus*.

Many people who practice in astrology believe that Ophiuchus is the unrecognised thirteenth star sign.

Also featured is the constellation of *Serpens* or "The Snake," who Asclepius witnessed bringing healing herbs to another snake who was sick, and this event started him on his discovery of benefits of medicinal herbs.

Planned launch 2026

Novella eight - the constellations of Cancer & Leo

Novella eight - the constellations of Cancer & Leo and the stories of Karkinos the giant crab, Zosma the Nemean lioness, Astron the hydra, Aquila the eagle, Sagitta the arrow, and the constellation named after Herakles the Demi-God.

The birth of Herakles was surrounded by controversy. Being the demi-god son of the King of all the gods, he found it difficult to live a routine life with his wife and children.

Herakles was persecuted by Hera for being her husband Zeus's illegitimate son, and so he was inflicted by incessant painful headaches. He was told of a remedy by the oracle in Delphi, but before he could be cured, it required him to agree to take on many incredible tasks which were assigned to him by the local king. By completing these labours, he should be able to go on to live a long and fulfilling life.

He later became immortal, and Herakles is forever remembered as a Greek Mythological hero for defeating the giant crab that became known as constellation "Cancer".

He also killed the man-eating lioness that became known as the constellation Leo. He slew the serpent of Lake Lerna, which is now known as the constellation "Hydra".

Herakles used an arrow now known as the constellation "Sagitta" to kill a giant eagle that became to be known as the constellation Aquila or "The Eagle".

Herakles was finally accepted at Mount Olympus and was honoured with the constellation Herakles also known as "Hercules".

This book is now available

Novella nine - the constellation Gemini

Novella nine - the constellation Gemini and the story of the twins, Castor and Polydeuces.

And the constellation The Swan or Cygnus.

Leucippe was desperate to become a grandmother. Fed up with her son-in-law's lack of progress, she asked Zeus for help. When Zeus arrived, he took the opportunity, disguised himself as a swan, and then he did much more than just arrange for Leda to become pregnant.

The Spartan twins grew up to become skilled horsemen, hunters, warriors, and adventurers. They embarked on many journeys together and their adventures included sailing on the Argo with Jason on his quest for the golden fleece, being hunters at the Calydonian wild boar hunt, and fighting Trojans at Troy. It was their sister Helen, who was the central reason for that protracted war.

The twins were honoured by Zeus for their bravery and commitment to each other, and he cast their image into the night sky to be forever remembered as the constellation of the Twins, which is now known as "*Gemini*". Also featured in this story is the constellation The Swan or "*Cygnus*".

This book is now available

Novella ten - the constellations of Virgo & Libra

Novella ten - the constellations of Virgo & Libra and the story of the Astraea the maiden, and Themis the scales.

Astraea and Themis were both goddesses who were committed to advancing the living conditions of the humans who lived on the island of Thera. Along with other gods and goddess they believed that they'd become the role models for all future human progress advancements.

Astraea strongly believed in justice and sort punishment for those that transgressed against the common good. Her belief was that punishment was a deterrent and that the formal process of trial and conviction for those found guilty of a crime had a place in society.

Themis was more about bringing about restitution to an aggrieved person who was treated unfairly by another. He mediation skills gave rise to the belief that there was always a remedy when agreements fell apart.

However, the speed of their progress and their intentions to achieve self-determination worried Zeus. After inspecting the work and assessing all that had been achieved, he concluded that it must come to an abrupt end. And as every Greek immortal knows, when Zeus is determined and has made up his mind, nothing stops it his decision from happening. For Astraea the decision was devastating, so she cast herself into the night sky as "the maiden", forever watching over humanity as the constellation **"Virgo"**.

Themis was later honoured for her balanced outlook on life and is remembered as the scales as she evenly balanced out her reasoning and decisions. She is now known to us as the constellation **"Libra"**.

This book is now available

Novella eleven – the constellation Aquarius

Novella eleven – the constellation Aquarius and the story of Ganymede the Water Bearer.

Ganymede was adopted by a family of shepherds when he was found abandoned as a young child. He preferred his own company, and whilst good at caring for the sheep he was regarded as a misfit by his adopted family.

One day, as he was tending the sheep, he was spotted by Zeus, who flying past in his eagle form. Out of curiosity Zeus landed to meet the young man and became quickly enamoured with him. Ganymede found himself attracted to the powerful God and very much wanted to be with him. Zeus easily convinced the young man to give up his shepherding life and come with him to Mount Olympus.

Ganymede became Zeus's friend and lover. He took over the role of cup bearer during important civil functions from Zeus's daughter Hebe, as she had found love and married a Greek Hero. Ganymede quickly became fascinated with aqueducts and fountains, and he was responsible for improving the water quality and availability of clean drinking water to Mount Olympus's inhabitants. His contribution is celebrated as the constellation of the "Water Bearer" now know to us as **"Aquarius"**.

This book is now available

Novella twelve – the constellation Sagittarius

Novella twelve – the constellation Sagittarius and the story of the "Archer" Crotus.

A water Naiad nymph named Eupheme was a demi-goddess of the Hippocrene freshwater spring near Mount Helicon. She was youthful, very beautiful, and powerful. She met and had a relationship with the God Pan, a Satyr, famous for playing the pipes was the god of shepherds, flocks, rustic musicians, and improvisation. Their romance led to the birth of Crotus.

Crotus was a Satyr and grew up to be like his like his father, preferring the company of muses. Most Satyrs preferred the company of Dionysus, God of wine, revelry, and debauchery, so Crotus was unusual in this way.

The muses were providers of inspiration to artists, musicians, poets, story tellers, artisans, entertainers, and dancers. They brought out the natural talents of those they inspired, and positively encouraged them to excel by pursuing their passions and striving for perfection in their chosen art form.

Crotus was also a great hunter, and many say that he invented the hunting bow. He was more popular as a musician and his most noteworthy contribution to performance music was the addition of rhythmic beats used to accompany the musician's musical score. He was also responsible for the introduction of a ritual applause to signify both pleasure from the performance and gratitude to the artist for their dedication to the composition and the quality of the performance. The applause was widely recognised as a significant motivator for artistic excellence.

Crotus was a mortal, and when he died, the Younger Muses petitioned Zeus to have his likeness immortalised as place in the night sky. Their petition was positively received, and, in his honour, he created the constellation of the Archer which is known to us as **Sagittarius**.

Planned launch 2026

Novella thirteen – the constellation Centaurus

Novella thirteen – the constellation Centaurus and the story of the tutor Cheiron.

Cheiron was a centaur who became the tutor to many of the legendary heroes of Greek mythology. Unlike other centaurs, Cheiron was intelligent, civilised and very kind. He was the teacher of students that included Jason, Castor, Polydeuces, Asclepius, Peleus, and Achilles and he taught them philosophy, archery, hunting, medicine, music, gymnastics, and the art of prophecy.

His life ended tragically when he was accidently struck with a poisoned arrow by his close friend, Herakles. Herakles had loosed the arrow in an attempt to ward off marauding cruel centaurs who came to cause mischief to Cheiron, but in the confusion, Cheiron stepped into the path of the arrow and was stuck. His immortality prevented his death, but the strong poison caused him everlasting agony. He decided to surrender his immortality to Zeus so that he could pass into the underworld. He was then commemorated as the constellation of the Centaur and is known to us as **Centaurus.**

Planned launch 2026

The other Greek constellations that are yet to be featured include Andromeda, Ara, Auriga, Boötes, Cassiopeia, Cepheus, Corona Australis, Corona Borealis, Corvus, Crater, Delphinus, Equuleus, Eridanus, Lepus, Lupus, Lyra, Pegasus, Perseus, Piscis, Austrinus, Triangulum, Ursa Major, Ursa Minor, and Argo Navis (now divided into Carina, Puppis, and Vela)

Follicle Farm – A novel adventure

Follicle Farm – A novel adventure.

Follicle Farm is a comical and imaginative insight into organisational structure and behaviour of the trillions of cells that make up the microscopic world of every living person. It reveals how cells within the human body really think and how they, mostly, work well together. Bobby is a Mitochondria, and he works as a humble Follicle Farmer. He, with millions of colleagues, are part of the amazing organisation dedicated to growing hair for the human male that they live inside of. Recently, Bobby made an important discovery when he learned how to reverse the effects of alopecia and greying hair. Now it's up to management to debate if they should use his technique.

Join Bobby as he travels the body, ably assisted by Banjo and Skip, as he meets and deals with other human cells in various systems throughout the body. Bobby quickly learns there is more to management than just servicing the body's needs. Cliques, quirks, politics, unions, and hidden agendas, all thrive in Bobby's world.

You'll share in his adventure of personal growth as he encourages other Follicle Farmers to utilises best practices in growing quality hair.

This book is now available

Your concise guide to the meaning of life

Your concise guide to the meaning of life.

(Non-Fiction)

This is a serious book designed to help people. Its main purpose is to assist you on how to gain insights on how to live a happier and more fulfilled life. It will give you, the reader, instant benefits. It is peppered with many great quotes, many of them are my own. I've combined my interest in philosophy, sociology, psychology, and history to delve into the true meaning of life. The reader will not only understand why they are here, but how to make their experience more meaningful.

My main aim is to inspire readers into taking more control of how they make decisions that positively affect their achievements, successes, happiness, and therefore their well-being. The book is a summary of concise points that are easy to learn and apply to the readers life for an immediate benefit. It includes popular relevant quotes to re-enforce the messages and teaching. I have also included personal anecdotes that give real life and meaningful examples of how the material applies to all readers.

Topics include

- an explanation the main purpose for living.
- how to improve your relationships.
- how communication works and how to
  make it more effective.
- understanding your needs and desires and
  how to improve outcomes for yourself.
- understanding what motivates other people.
- how to exceed your own expectations.
- understanding your own personal legal,
  moral, ethical, and value system.
- improving your control over your emotions.
- understanding the concepts of faith,
  fate and fairness.
- and being better prepared for the
  final stages of your life.

This book is now available

www.ingramcontent.com/pod-product-compliance
Lightning Source LLC
Chambersburg PA
CBHW070948180726
48291CB00004B/1187